Dear Reader,

The wacky and wonderful Morelli family, whom you met and grew to love in *Staying Single*, the book that launched the Flipside line, is back and more engaging than ever. Or so I think!

This time it's Lisa Morelli's heart that's in jeopardy. This wild, unconventional woman must decide if her soon-to-be ex-husband, Alexander Mackenzie, is her Prince Charming or just another frog she's kissed while trying to find the man of her dreams. And being married to the guy just seems to be complicating the issue.

Of course, Lisa's mom, the ever formidable and interfering Josephine, is on hand to guide her daughter down the primrose path to happiness. It's what mothers do, after all!

As always, I would love to hear your comments on *Suddenly Single*. Please write to me at P.O. Box 41206, Fredericksburg, VA 22404, or visit my Web site at www.milliecriswell.com.

Best always,

Millie Criswell

"What on earth are you doing here, Lisa? Is Mom okay?"

"Why does everyone think there's something wrong with Mom? That woman will outlive us all, Francie, and you know it." Lisa sighed. "Mom's fine. I'm the one with the problem."

Francie looked meaningfully at her husband, who took the hint. "I've got work to do," he said before kissing his wife on the cheek and flashing her a smile full of promise. "Don't be too long, okay?"

After her brother-in-law had left, Lisa made gagging sounds, then said, "You two are going to make me throw up, if you're not careful. Are you always like this? So sickeningly sweet, lovey-dovey and moony-eyed? I feel like I'm developing diabetes just being in the same room with you two *sweethearts*."

Francie grinned and said, "We're newlyweds. What do you expect? I'm sure you and Alex behave exactly the same way. I'd bet money on it, in fact."

Not anymore, Lisa thought. "You'd lose. Alex and I have split. We're *kaput*, done, *finito*. Turns out I'm not the marrying kind after all."

Millie Criswell

Suddenly
Single

HARLEQUIN®

TORONTO • NEW YORK • LONDON
AMSTERDAM • PARIS • SYDNEY • HAMBURG
STOCKHOLM • ATHENS • TOKYO • MILAN • MADRID
PRAGUE • WARSAW • BUDAPEST • AUCKLAND

ISBN 0-373-44195-9

SUDDENLY SINGLE

ABOUT THE AUTHOR

Millie Criswell, *USA TODAY* bestselling author and winner of a *Romantic Times* Career Achievement Award and a National Readers Choice Award, has published over twenty-five romance novels. She began her writing career when her husband uttered those prophetic words: "Why don't you try writing one of those romances you're always reading?" Knowing that her dream of tap dancing with the Rockettes wasn't likely to materialize—due to a lack of dancing talent—Millie jumped on the idea with both feet, so to speak, and has been charming readers with hilarious stories and sparkling characters ever since. Millie resides in Virginia with her husband and her lovable Boston terrier.

Books by Millie Criswell

Don't miss any of our special offers. Write to us at the following address for information on our newest releases.

Harlequin Reader Service
U.S.: 3010 Walden Ave., P.O. Box 1325, Buffalo, NY 14269
Canadian: P.O. Box 609, Fort Erie, Ont. L2A 5X3

To my brilliant and wonderful editor,
Wanda Ottewell, who is such a joy to work with

1

THE POSSIBILITY of pregnancy loomed ugly on the horizon for Lisa Morelli, as she knocked on her sister's apartment door.

Of course, Lisa knew her mother would be thrilled if it turned out that she was pregnant. The only thing in life Josephine Morelli wanted more than seeing her two daughters wed was to get her hands on a grandchild. Girl or boy, it didn't matter, as long as it was healthy and had ten toes and fingers, though she would probably take the nine-toed variety if push came to shove.

Her mother's fixation on grandchildren was similar to the one she had about fiancés. Finding the perfect mate for Lisa gave her mother a purpose in life, but tended to make everyone else nuts.

Her mother's only criterion for potential bridegrooms was that they had to be breathing. And some of the old geezers Josephine had paraded before Lisa barely even met that standard.

Morris Parker, her parents' ancient accountant, carted an oxygen tank around with him wherever he went. Lisa had no doubt that it would have followed him into the bedroom, as well.

Not that she was interested. *There was something very unappealing about shriveled skin!*

Lisa's sister would also be elated if Lisa was to find herself pregnant. Francie had been counting the days, and her birth control pills, until she and her new husband Mark Fielding could begin a family. But since they'd only been married a few months, the couple had opted to wait a while longer, which seemed quite sensible to Lisa.

One never knew when one's marriage was going to end up in the shitter.

Nope. The only one who would have a conniption fit—*translation: suicidal tendencies*—if she was to find out she was pregnant was Lisa.

And not because she wasn't married.

But because she was—to Alexander Hamilton Mackenzie, her mama's boy, wimp-of-a-husband—wimp-of-a-*handsome-smart-great-giver-of-sex*-husband, she amended.

Her soon-to-be *ex*-husband, if Lisa Morelli Mackenzie had anything to say about it, and she most certainly did. Plenty, in fact!

Marrying Alex had been a huge mistake—one of many she'd made over the years. Lisa had always been impulsive and foolish when it came to men, and falling hard for Alex had been in keeping with her poor judgment.

Lisa hadn't expected to fall in love with the conservative mortgage banker. They were as different as night and day. But when she'd spotted him across the dance floor at Club Zero dressed in a three-piece business suit, no less, and looking totally out of place, her heart had begun hammering and had never stopped. He'd obviously felt the same attraction, for three weeks later they'd eloped and moved to Florida to live with his parents—her second biggest mistake.

Every time she thought about how Alex had tried to placate his snotty, upper-crud parents she went ballistic. She didn't display her Italian temperament very often, but when she got mad... Watch out! And she was mad as hell at Alex for what he had put her through. The Mackenzies made Bonnie and Clyde look like Ozzie and Harriet!

No. Discovering that she was pregnant would not be a good thing right now. *If ever.* Timing was everything, and hers...well, hers sucked! Always had and probably always would.

Besides, she doubted she would make a very good mother. She was too self-absorbed to share the spotlight with a baby, still too much of a child herself. At least, that's what her parents had been telling Lisa for years, and she was beginning to believe them.

Trying to please Josephine and John Morelli—impossible, in her opinion—was what had gotten her into this mess in the first place.

Lisa hadn't taken enough time to get to know Alex before marrying him. She'd only been dating him for a few weeks before agreeing to run off to that hideous wedding chapel in Las Vegas—her choice, not his.

Alex was much too conservative to ever suggest such an outlandish thing.

The man ironed his boxers, for chrissake!

The minister—she used that term loosely—who had performed the wedding ceremony and his wife were former circus performers. They had conducted the proceedings while riding unicycles and juggling oranges back and forth between them.

Alex had been hit on the right side of the head in a ride-by fruiting after reciting his "I dos" and had nearly been knocked unconscious, which would have proven disastrous for their wedding night—a truly memorable event, as it turned out.

Lisa had taken precautions against getting pregnant. Condoms had been the dress of the day, and night. Of course, she knew condoms weren't one hundred percent foolproof, but then, only abstinence was, and abstaining from having sex with Alexander would have been too Herculean a task for a mere mortal—*horny*—woman, such as herself.

Sex with Alex had been fabulous, delicious, the best ever. It was what made her lose whatever sense she'd been born with—according to her father, that hadn't been much—and toss caution to the wind.

John Morelli had a low opinion of his youngest daughter's ability to act rationally, and she certainly hadn't disproved that notion by eloping on impulse. Her parents had been furious when they'd found out what she'd done, especially after discovering that the bridegroom was a non-Catholic, non-Italian, WASP-white-bread mortgage banker.

Her hormones had always tended to get her into trouble.

Upon reflection, it also probably hadn't been a good idea to have had sex with Alex the night before she'd packed her bags, said goodbye to her witch-of-a-mother-in-law's Florida estate and hightailed it back to Philadelphia, brokenhearted and alone, but much wiser.

The one and only positive thing she had to show for her three-month marriage to Alexander Hamilton Mackenzie, besides the fabulous sex, was a great tan.

At least, she hoped that was all.

Banishing her disturbing thoughts, Lisa knocked on her sister's apartment door again. When there was still no answer, she cursed beneath her breath.

Lisa knew a lot of curse words; she was her mother's daughter, after all. They didn't call Josephine Morelli "The Terminator" for nothing!

After spending one night under her parents' roof listening to her mother wail about what a selfish, thoughtless daughter she had, Lisa was desperate for a place to stay and had come begging in the hope Francie would put her up for a few days, until she could find a job and get a place of her own.

She hated asking her sister for help, especially since Francie was a newlywed, but Lisa was quickly running out of options, not to mention money.

"She's not home. Francie and Mark took a couple of

days off and drove to Bucks County to look at houses. They left last night after work."

Turning, Lisa found her sister's former roommate, Leo Bergmann, standing behind her. The blond man, who reminded her of a young Elton John, sexual persuasion and all, was holding a bag of groceries and smiling that friendly, welcoming smile he always wore whenever he saw her.

"Hey, Leo! Do you know when Francie'll be back from big bucks country?"

Bucks County, land of stone farmhouses, quaint bed-and-breakfasts and assorted artsy types, was only a short drive from Philadelphia. Buying a house or property there definitely took big bucks, but her sister's husband worked for the Associated Press as a photojournalist so she knew they'd be able to afford it, if they were lucky enough to find a house they both could agree on.

Leo shrugged. "Sunday night, I suppose. Why?" His eyes filled with concern as he took in her bedraggled appearance. "You look awful, sweetie. Has something happened? Is it your mother?"

Lisa looked down at her soiled T-shirt and rumpled jeans. She hadn't had time to do laundry for a few days. No surprise there! She was not domestic goddess material.

"Hell, no! That woman's healthier than the proverbial horse. On second thought, it's sort of about my mother, but it has nothing to do with her health. Josephine's skill is in making others sick."

Leo, who knew Lisa and Francie's mother quite well—he'd been maid of honor at Francie's wedding—nodded absently in agreement. "I heard you got married. Where's your new husband? I've been dying to meet him. Francie tells me he's quite the hunk."

Lisa sighed, feeling tired and alone.

Damn you, Alex! Why didn't you love me enough?

"It's a long story, Leo."

"I've got the time, and..." He pulled a bottle of wine from his grocery sack and grinned enticingly.

She finally smiled back. "Why not? I can use some good *vino.*" Maybe it would drown the pain she was feeling. And Leo always had the best vintages to choose from. He was a collector of fine wines and had a pretty impressive cellar, though it wasn't really a cellar in the traditional sense, but a closet that had been converted into one, with temperature control and pretty redwood racks. "Got any of those sugared nuts I'm wild about?"

The blond man grinned. "Of course. I just stocked up." He nodded at the brown bag he was holding. "Three cans."

"Why aren't you and Francie working today? I thought you were trying to get that new business of yours off the ground." Leo had recently started his own interior design firm and had hired her sister to assist him, after she'd been fired from her previous job as a publicist.

Francie had a knack for landing on her feet, and Lisa

envied her sister that. She usually landed on her rear, stuck like a too big butt in a too small toilet seat.

Following Leo to his apartment door, she waited while he unlocked it. "Designing Women is doing great. Francie's been a huge help. I'm so fortunate to have her working with me. But today's Saturday, in case you haven't noticed, and the store's not open on Saturday. Francie thought we should be, but I had to draw the line at that. Weekends are for partying."

How could she have forgotten it was Saturday? Like her marriage, her mind must be going down the shitter, as well.

"You're my kind of man, Leo. Always have been."

"Well, sweetie, if I ever decide to go straight you'll be the first woman I call now that Francie's married. Oh wait, you're married, too. Damn!"

"Not for long."

His eyes widened. "Oh?"

They entered the living room of the apartment, where Leo filled two wineglasses with a full-bodied Cabernet Sauvignon and handed Lisa one, then they both plopped down on opposite ends of the red leather sofa.

"Do tell? And don't leave out any of the gory stuff. It's been boring since Francie left. I've had absolutely no one to gossip with at night."

Lisa sipped her wine thoughtfully. "I guess I shouldn't have rushed into marriage, Leo. I was stupid, didn't really think about what it might entail, like having to put up with Alex's family, who are a total nightmare."

A major understatement, if ever there was one.

"So the problem isn't with Alex, but with his family?"

"He's to blame, too. Alex didn't stand up for me, or take my side in anything. He just let that old bitch walk all over me and insult me."

And she would never forgive him for that. If there was one thing Lisa was, it was loyal, and she expected the same degree of loyalty in return.

"Miriam hated me on sight. I thought in time I could win her over. Ha! That was a good one. The woman makes Leona Helmsley look like a saint." *The Queen of Meaner*, Lisa thought.

"Miriam objected to everything about me. She particularly didn't like the way I dressed and was always calling me a hippie, which I think was a euphemistic way to say hooker. She insisted on taking me shopping, tried to make me buy clothes that not even my mother would be caught dead in. I'm not kidding, Leo. All her friends dressed so ultraconservatively, they looked like the Stepford wives come to life—monogrammed blouses with matching monogrammed purses, wraparound skirts, that sort of thing." She shuddered at the thought.

"Sort of a *Night of the Living Dead* look, huh?"

"Exactly. When I refused to go along, she told me I was being selfish, that I was an embarrassment to Alex."

"That was cruel."

"Yeah, but not as cruel as her wanting me to chop off my hair and dye it blond, so I'd fit in better."

Leo's eyes widened. "That gorgeous dark hair? You're kidding."

"Afraid not."

"What about Alex's father? Was he awful, too?"

"Rupert, the magnificent?" Lisa shook her head and heaved a sigh, remembering all the glares and the disappointed looks the older man had cast her way. "The same, though not quite as vocal.

"The Mackenzies are very wealthy. They had a different image of what Alex's wife should be—white Anglo-Saxon Protestant, to be exact. And being a Southerner wouldn't have hurt.

"The fact that I was Italian and Catholic went against me from the beginning. They hated the way I dressed, talked, breathed. They hated pretty much everything about me. Guess I didn't meet their exacting standards. I doubt anyone could."

Miriam had actually expected Lisa to wear white gloves to one of the tea parties she held for her lady friends. And Lisa had complied. *Sort of.* She'd worn elbow-length white gloves, accompanied by a sequined crop top. Lisa had known it would piss off her mother-in-law, but by that point she hadn't really given a damn.

"I'm sorry, sweetie. That must have been tough. I know what it's like not to meet expectations. People can be quite cruel. What are you going to do now?"

"Get a divorce, as soon as I can afford a lawyer." Which, admittedly, could take a while, finances being what they were—nonexistent.

"Are you working?"

Lisa shook her head. "I tried to get my old job back at the bookstore, but they'd already hired someone else." Actually, the manager of Carlton Books had looked horrified at the prospect of hiring Lisa back.

Dick Lester, or Dick *Less*, as she liked to call him, sure as hell hadn't minded pinching her butt whenever he got the chance. One day when she'd finally had enough of his sexist treatment, she'd punched the disgusting pig in the balls, thus ending her lackluster career as a bookseller and his as Philadelphia's oldest living stud muffin.

"I'm afraid I'm not qualified to do much, Leo, which is my biggest problem." Lisa hated working regular hours and conforming to other people's rules and regulations. Being an adult sucked, for the most part, which is why she hadn't been too successful at holding down a job for more than a few months at a time.

Leo reached for his wallet. "I can lend you some money if—"

Lisa shook her head adamantly. "No, Leo! That's very kind of you, but I won't take your money." Aside from his design-firm income, Leo lived off a trust fund left to him by his deceased parents. He was generous to a fault, and Lisa drew the line at accepting his money.

"I still have a little cash left to tide me over until I can find a job. What I need is a place to live. I will not spend one more night under my mother's roof. That woman is a nightmare. Can you believe she accused me of trying to ruin her life?"

An impossibility, since Lisa was too busy ruining her own.

Leo refilled their glasses and set the bottle of wine back down on the coffee table, and being careful to use a coaster. "From nightmarish mother-in-law to nightmarish mother in one fell swoop, huh?"

"Something like that. I was hoping to find Francie home, so I could beg a room for a few days." Lisa sipped her wine thoughtfully, wondering if she had enough cash for a cheap hotel room. Her credit cards were maxed to the hilt, due to the exorbitant airfare she'd purchased at the last minute to fly home from Florida. Of course, at that point she'd have paid any amount of money to leave Alex and his family. In fact, she would have walked home.

"But she's just married, sweetie. I doubt Mark would be thrilled by that idea. And you couldn't really blame him. Third wheels suck when you're in love and doing the dirty on a regular basis."

Lisa nodded, knowing what Leo said was true. As in love as Francie was with Mark, and vice versa, she doubted the couple would welcome her into their love nest with open arms. "Well, I'll live on the street before going back to my parents' house. It's only January. It can't be that cold at night."

Leo looked horrified by her suggestion. "Don't be

stupid! You can bunk here until Francie gets back. Her old room is still pretty much intact."

Breathing a huge sigh of relief, Lisa smiled gratefully. "Are you sure, Leo? I wouldn't want to put you out or anything."

It was a bald-faced lie. She might not take his money, but Lisa didn't mind putting Leo out, circumstances being what they were. She didn't relish using Leo, or anyone else for that matter, but Lisa was an opportunist, and if an opportunity presented itself, she'd be foolish not to act on it.

"It'll only be for a couple of days, right? So you won't be putting me out."

"Right," Lisa agreed, but her mind was already working overtime, trying to figure out how to turn temporary into permanent.

"I WANT YOU to stop packing that suitcase right now, young man, and think about what you're doing."

Alex's gaze lifted to his mother. Miriam Mackenzie was still an attractive woman, though the former Miss Mint Julep was definitely starting to show her age. She'd been looking tired and wrinkled lately, despite her many face-lifts and the strawberry-blond hair color from an expensive salon to hide the gray.

He used to tease his mother that she could give Michael Jackson a run for his money in the plastic-surgery department, which had never gone over well. His mother didn't have a sense of humor when it came to her fading looks.

Alex and his mother had always shared a close relationship, though at times she was smothering and bossy, like now. Still, as much as he loved her, he loved his wife more.

"I've thought a great deal about what I'm doing, Mother, and I'm leaving. I've got to try and win Lisa back. I love her, and I don't want to live my life without her."

Clearly distressed, Miriam walked farther into her son's room and took a seat on the edge of the antique tester bed, folding her hands primly in her lap, as any good Southern woman was wont to do. Her voice softened. "Lisa isn't right for you, Alex. She doesn't fit into our...*your* way of life. I thought that had become quite apparent these past few months. You can't turn a sow's ear into a silk purse, as the saying goes. Lord knows we tried."

Alex's voice reflected his anger. "What's apparent is that I'm a fool. I know Lisa isn't perfect or acceptable by your standards, Mother, but she's perfect for me. She's like a breath of fresh air. You and father never took the time to really get to know her. If you had, you would have loved her as much as I do."

"But she has no social graces, Alex. Surely you realize that. She balked at every opportunity—to purchase a more appropriate wardrobe, to have dance lessons so we could take her to the country club, to—"

"You tried to change her. I don't know why I was so blind in seeing what your motives were from the beginning. I never should have brought her here, I can see that now. We were happy in Philadelphia. We should have just stayed there."

Miriam stood, a steely look of determination on her face. "That wasn't the real world, Alexander—your world. You come from wealth and privilege. Nothing, including a change of geography, is going to change what you are or where you come from."

"Well, maybe I need to change. I'm not saying that I'm not grateful for everything you and Father have given me—the excellent Ivy League education and the opportunity to work in the family banking business. But it's time I became my own man, made my own mistakes."

"You've certainly done that, son, now haven't you?"

Pausing in his packing, Alex looked back over his shoulder to find his father standing there. Gray-haired, broad-shouldered and as intimidating as ever, Rupert Mackenzie was a formidable force in the world of banking and commerce—and in his own family. And though Alex loved his father, loved both his parents, he wasn't about to let them ruin his life.

He'd already done a good job of that himself.

"I'm twenty-nine years old. It's high time I made my own mistakes. And I don't consider having married Lisa to be one. You and Mother were very hard on her, criticizing every little thing she said or did. I tried to keep silent, to avoid confrontation, in the hope that you'd accept her in time. I never expected you to chase her away."

"A woman with backbone wouldn't have been

scared off like a frightened rabbit, Alex. You know that as well as I do.''

Zipping his black-leather carry-on bag shut, Alex stood up and faced both his parents. "Lisa's got more courage than most people I know. She's not afraid of the world, hasn't been cosseted and fawned over like a favored family pet, as I have. And she's managed to survive, to do all right for herself. I admire that about her. I love her. And I intend to have her for my wife, one way or another.''

"Tread carefully, son. There's a lot at stake that you could be throwing away.''

Eyes narrowed, Alex stared down his father. "If you're threatening me with my inheritance, don't bother. I know enough about the mortgage-banking business to start my own firm, and I doubt I'll have any trouble finding a job in Philadelphia. Now that my assignment there has ended for Mackenzie Enterprises, I'm free to pursue my own interests.''

"Are you resigning from the firm?" Alex's father looked shocked, which was a shock in itself. Few things ever threw the old man. "I built that firm as a legacy for you.''

"It appears that I am." And no one was more surprised about that than Alex.

Miriam stepped forward, placing her hand on Alex's arm, and looking beseechingly at her husband. "You're our only son, Alex, and we love you. We have only your best interests at heart. Surely you know that.

Please don't make a rash decision that could ruin your future."

"What I know is that I'm in love with Lisa and have been from the first moment I laid eyes on her across a crowded dance floor. I'm determined to win her back, no matter what I have to do. And trust me, knowing what her family is like, that won't be easy."

His mother grew alarmed. "Why? Are the Morellis connected to the Mafia? Are you in danger?"

Alex would have laughed, if he thought his mother was joking. Sadly, she wasn't. "Not every Italian-American is a member of the mob, Mother. The Morellis are hardworking, upstanding people. I don't think they're related to the Sopranos."

"But you don't know them that well."

"I know their daughter, and that tells me all I want to know."

Alex picked up his bag and headed for the door.

"You'll regret this, son, if you walk out that door," his father warned.

"And I'll regret it the rest of my life if I don't."

2

LISA HAD BEEN WAITING anxiously all weekend for her sister's return, so when she heard Francie's voice on Leo's voice mail Sunday night, letting him know that she and Mark were back, Lisa hightailed it down the hallway to Francie's apartment.

Mark answered the door, looking tired, well kissed and as disgustingly handsome as ever. Apparently the trip to Buck's County had gone well, or else he and Francie had just engaged in a round of fabulous sex.

She rather thought it was the latter.

"Lisa, this is a surprise! What are you doing here? I thought you were in Florida."

"Sorry to intrude, Mark, but I need to talk to Francie. It's about why I'm not in Florida—a long sad story, and one I'd rather not tell twice, if you don't mind." One she'd rather not tell at all, if she were truthful with herself, but Francie was going to ask probing questions and would expect direct answers.

Though Francie was only two years older than Lisa, she took her job as big sister seriously. But then, Francie took most things seriously. She was the reliable, conscientious, mostly well-behaved daughter, while

Lisa was the screwup. Her present situation was testament to that.

"Sure, come on in. Francie's in the shower. She'll just be a few more minutes. Let's have a beer. I'll tell you about our trip to Buck's County. We spent the weekend looking at houses and we think we've found the one we want, if we can get our price. The sellers seem anxious, so we're keeping our fingers crossed."

"That's great!" Following her brother-in-law into the kitchen, Lisa seated herself at the table, accepting the frosty beer mug he handed her. "I can't wait to hear all about it. Did you take lots of pictures?" Mark's eyebrow shot up in disbelief, and Lisa shook her head. "Stupid question to ask a photographer, huh?"

"I took several rolls of film, but I haven't had a chance to develop them yet. Francie took some nice shots with the digital camera, but I won't steal her thunder. She'll want to show you those herself."

Wrapped in a blue terry cloth bathrobe, Francie stepped into the kitchen at that moment, her smile melting into concern when she spotted her younger sister. "I thought I heard voices. What on earth are you doing here, Lisa? Is it Mom? Is she okay?"

"Why does everyone always think there's something wrong with Mom? That woman is going to outlive us all." Lisa sighed. "Mom's fine. I'm the one with the problem."

Francie looked meaningfully at her husband, who was wise enough to take the hint. "I've got work to do," he said, "so I'll say good-night." Mark kissed his wife's cheek, flashing her a smile full of promise. "Don't be too long, okay?"

After her brother-in-law departed, Lisa stuck her finger down her throat and made gagging sounds. "You two are going to make me throw up, if you're not careful. Are you always like this?" She shook her head, a bemused smile lighting her face.

"Like what?"

"Sickeningly sweet, lovey-dovey, moony-eyed and horny as rabbits? I feel like I'm developing diabetes just being in the same room with you two sweethearts."

Used to her sister's outrageous remarks, Francie merely grinned. "We're newlyweds. What do you expect? I'm sure you and Alex behave in exactly the same way. I'd bet money on it, in fact."

Not anymore, Lisa thought. "You'd lose. Alex and I have split. We're kaput, done, *finito*."

"What?" Francie dropped into the chair across from her sister, a stunned look on her face. "What happened? I thought you two were madly in love with each other."

"Love wasn't the problem, and neither was sex, which was fabulous, I might add. It was his parents. Alex changed once we got to Florida and began living with them." Lisa detailed her treatment at Miriam and Rupert Mackenzie's hands. "When he refused to stand up for me, I got fed up and left."

"But to leave without telling anyone, Lisa. They must be frantic with worry."

Lisa laughed, though there was no humor in it. "I haven't heard a peep from anyone, including Alex." And that hurt; it hurt a lot. After all, she had a cell phone. Of course, the battery was dead, and it had only been a couple of days, but still...

"I guess he must realize, as I do, that our marriage was a huge mistake. I'm sure he's relieved as hell that I left. It saved him the trouble of kicking me out."

Francie reached out to clasp her sister's hand. "I'm sure that's not true, Lisa. And you shouldn't think such things. Alex loves you. I'm positive of that."

"How do you know? You only met him that one time, right before we moved to Florida."

"Because I saw the way he looked at you. You can't pretend love. It was there in his eyes, for all the world to see."

"Oh, pleeze! You are going to make me throw up. I doubt there's any such thing as love. Okay, maybe you and Mark have the genuine thing. I'm not sure what Alex and I experienced, probably lust. After all, the sex was fabulous—but you can't expect sex to make up for all that was lacking in our relationship."

Francie arched a skeptical eyebrow. "Such as?"

"We have nothing in common. Alex comes from money, oodles of it. He's never experienced hard knocks, rejection or parental disapproval. He works for his father's company; they think he walks on water."

"So what's wrong with that? Lots of children work for their parents."

"The Mackenzies' blood isn't blue, France, it's positively green, as in greenbacks. They're into all sorts of social activities, like the country club and yachting. Hell, I can't even swim. I nearly drowned in the kiddy pool at the club. Miriam was not pleased."

"But you knew about the differences between you and Alex before you married him. You knew he was a mortgage banker and a great deal more conservative than you could ever hope to be. In fact, I worried at your decision to elope. Alex was definitely different from the other men you'd dated."

Lisa was thoughtful for a moment as she sipped her beer. "I guess I wanted to impress Mom and Dad, be the kind of daughter they wanted. You were getting married to Mark, and I wanted to share in some of the adoration and attention. Pathetic, huh?"

Francie sighed, concern for her sister etched on her face. "Oh, Lisa..."

"Or maybe I thought I had fallen in love and wasn't paying attention to the differences in our personalities and upbringing. I don't really know. I just know I screwed up. Big-time."

"What do you intend to do?"

"Well, originally I was going to ask you for a place to stay until I could get things worked out financially, but then Leo pointed out that might not be a very good idea, so I've been staying at his apartment all weekend, trying to come up with a plan."

Eyes widening, Francie said, "You and Leo? Now there's an odd couple if there ever was one."

Offended, Lisa stiffened. "What do you mean?"

"Leo is a compulsive neat freak. Your messy ways will drive him nuts."

"Oh that." She waved away her sister's objection with a flick of her wrist. "He's already made a few comments about water rings on the table and toothpaste caps being left off. Jeez! Leo's worse than Mom."

"How long are you going to live there?"

"Leo's offer is only good for the weekend, but I'm hoping he'll give me a permanent place to stay after he sees how well we get on. I'm trying to impress him."

"With what? You don't clean. You don't know a thing about wine. And I don't need to point out that you're the wrong sex."

Lisa made a face. "Like Leo, I like to party and have a good time. And we share a love of toffee peanuts, not to mention that I'm a big Cher fan."

"Yes, you and Leo are well suited in that way." Francie shook her head. "I'm not sure, however, that peanuts and parties will be enough to lure him to your way of thinking, Lisa. It takes him a while to warm up to people."

"Maybe you can help. Put in a good word for me."

"I'll see what I can do, but don't expect me to work miracles. Leo knows you better than you think."

Lisa brightened instantly. "That should go in my favor then, right?"

Clearing her throat, Francie hesitated, then nodded. "Uh, yeah, right."

ALEX DROPPED his black leather carry-on bag in the front hallway of Bill Connor's Philadelphia apartment, where he'd arranged to stay temporarily.

Bill was his former college roommate, and they'd always gotten along well, sharing similar views on politics, movies and music. The one thing they differed on was women—Alex admired them; Bill consumed them.

"I really appreciate your putting me up, Bill. It's been a long time since Harvard."

"What are old roommates for?" the lawyer said, nodding toward the kitchen. "Come on in, your room's all ready. I admit I was surprised when you called out of the blue last night. It's been what, three years since our last college reunion?"

"Four, actually. Time flies when you're having fun," Alex said, sarcasm edging his words.

Lisa had only been gone three days, and he missed her like crazy. He'd fought the urge to phone, to beg her to come back...fearing what her answer would be. He'd come to Philadelphia so he could reason with her, show her how much he loved and wanted her back.

Grabbing two Bud Lights from the refrigerator, Bill handed Alex one and they headed into the living room, which reeked of Pottery Barn and Restoration Hardware. Alex took a seat on the big brown-leather recliner.

"And have you been having fun, buddy?"

"I did for a while. I got married a few months back." And it had been fun—fun, fantastic and fabulous.

What the hell had happened?

"No shit! That's great. Congratulations! Who's the lucky lady?"

"Her name's Lisa...Lisa Morelli. But...she's left me."

"No shit! That sucks. For another guy? I'm sorry as hell, Alex." Bill patted his friend's arm consolingly. "If you need a good lawyer, let me know. I've got lots of experience in these matters."

Alex shook his head and sidestepped the topic of divorce. "I'm not exactly sure of the reason for Lisa leaving like she did. She just packed up and split in the middle of the night, no note, no explanation. The bed was empty when I awoke the next morning." And after they'd made such glorious love, and she'd told him how much she adored him—it had added insult to injury.

"Pardon me for saying so, Alex, but this woman sounds like an insensitive bitch. You might have dodged a bullet on this one. Trust me, I know what I'm talking about."

Heaving a sigh, Alex replied, "That's just it. Lisa's not a bitch. She's great. She's impulsive, I'll admit that. But she's not the type to purposely hurt someone."

"So why did she leave then?"

"My guess is that it had something to do with my parents' treatment of her. You know how snobbish they can be. They never accepted Lisa, never thought she was good enough for me, and they let her know it, in many subtle and not so subtle ways.

"Maybe she got tired of their rudeness." Alex shook his head. "I don't know for sure because she never complained or said a word. I know now that I should have stepped in and tried to smooth things out, but I was hoping they would resolve their differences once they got to know each other better."

"Man, it's tough when your parents are involved. There's that whole divided loyalties thing to consider."

"But that's just it, Bill. My loyalties weren't...aren't divided. I'm on Lisa's side, but I guess I never let her know that, not really, not like I should have. I screwed up, royally."

"Yeah, well after you've been married a time or two you figure these things out."

Alex's eyes widened. "Are you telling me that you're divorced? Hell, I'm embarrassed to admit that I didn't even know you were married."

With his sandy hair, deep blue eyes and dimpled smile, Bill had always been popular with the girls at school. He flitted from one relationship to the next, never tying himself down long enough to get serious about anyone in particular. So to find out his friend had been married, not once, but twice, came as quite a shock to Alex.

"It was brief—they both were. Each one of my marriages lasted less than a year. I wasn't good at the whole matrimony thing."

Alex sipped his beer, then said, "I'm sorry to hear that. Are you dating anyone now?"

"Yeah." Bill grinned. "Annie's a flight attendant. She's gone a lot, which works out good for both of us.

That way we don't get on each other's nerves. I like her a lot, but I like my space even more."

"I miss Lisa like crazy. I want her back. I'll do anything to make that happen."

Bill's lawyerly instincts came rushing to the forefront. "Whoa, buddy! Don't start talking like that, or she'll have you by the balls before you know what hit you."

"I don't care. Lisa's the only thing in this world that matters to me. I just wish I'd let her know that. She probably hates me now, probably thinks I'm as shallow as my parents."

"It's hard to know what a woman's thinking, Alex. I find it's easier not to even try. It's just too damn frustrating. And being men, we usually end up guessing wrong anyway."

Alex shrugged, wondering if his friend was right.

"The Eagles are playing the Washington Redskins tonight at nine. Let's order in some Chinese and drown our sorrow in a few dozen beers while we watch the game. Things might be clearer in the morning when you're not so tired."

Alex nodded. He was tired and confused and hurt. And he had no answers for any of the unsettling questions that kept popping into his mind.

The only thing he knew for sure was that Lisa was gone, and he had to figure out a way to get her back. How he was going to do that, he wasn't certain. He knew only that his future happiness depended on it.

"WHAT DO YOU MEAN, you're going to look for an apartment? You're married. Have you forgotten? Mar-

ried women live with their husbands. And they
don't live with other men, even if those men are *fa-
nooks*.''

At times like this, Lisa wondered why she visited her
mother. It was too early in the morning to be driven insane, and Josephine definitely made her crazy with her
unwanted opinions and advice. But after her talk with
Francie the previous evening, she'd had the strongest
urge to see her mom.

Now, of course, she wished she had just taken an en-
ema and gotten whatever it was out of her system.

Lisa gulped down the strong, black liquid that her
mother tried to pass off as coffee and replied, ''I told
you, Mom, Alex and I are through. I'm not going to live
with a man who doesn't respect me and is tied to his
mother's apron strings. I didn't know when I married
Alex that I was marrying a mama's boy.''

''How could you know? You barely knew the man.''

Lisa winced at the truth of her mother's words.

''And so what if he shows respect? What's wrong
with that? A son should respect his mother. Look at
your brother. Jack's crazy about me. He's a good boy,
your brother.''

''First of all, Jack is a teenager and should still be tied
to your apron strings. Alex, on the other hand, is a
grown man—a grown *married* man. He should have
cleaved to his wife, like the Bible says. Go ask Father
Scaletti if you don't believe me.''

Josephine was of the opinion that everything that

came out of the parish priest's mouth was gospel, so Lisa figured she might as well use it to bolster her case.

"For someone who rarely goes to church, it surprises me that you would know what the Bible says." Josephine took her daughter's hand, her tone softening.

"Why must you make everything so difficult, Lisa? You made vows with this man. Now you must try and work it out between you. Just because something isn't perfect doesn't mean you should throw it away.

"Marriage takes work. No one said it was easy. You think your father and I didn't have our share of problems over the years? We did. But we stuck it out, for better or worse."

Lisa heaved a dispirited sigh. "I knew you wouldn't take my side, Mom. You never do. Now if it were Francie having the problem, things would be different. You always stand up for her."

"Your sister uses her head before she rushes into things."

"You mean before she rushes out of the church, don't you? I hope you're not forgetting the three failed wedding attempts you paid for before Mark Fielding came along to hog-tie and drag Francie to the altar."

"I'm not saying your sister can't be stubborn, but most of the time Francie listens, something you don't do. You think you know everything.

"I tried to tell you that the kind of men you were dating were wrong for you. Who dates a female impersonator? Tell me that? But would you listen? And now that you've found a normal one, you want to get rid of him." Exasperated, Josephine slapped her hand to her forehead.

"If you met his parents, you wouldn't think Alex was normal."

"I spoke to his mother on the phone, after you told us you had eloped. She's a cold fish, that woman. I could tell right away. But I'm sure she loves her son the way I love you and wants him to be happy."

Lisa rolled her eyes. "Oh yeah. Miriam wants Alex to be happy, just not with me. She doesn't think I'm good enough for him, Ma. And his father feels the same way."

Upon hearing that, Josephine let loose a string of curses, and then crossed herself to atone for her sin. "What is this woman, Mussolini, that she thinks my daughter isn't good enough? I should call her up and give her a piece of my mind."

"It wouldn't do any good. Honey oozes out of Miriam Mackenzie's sweet Southern belle mouth. She looks right at you and smiles, and then pushes a knife into your back. I've got so many holes I should be leaking like a sieve."

From the start, Miriam had gone out of her way to cause trouble between Lisa and Alex. The woman was always bringing her son's old girlfriends into the conversation, going on about how accomplished they were, how beautiful, how much Alex had adored them, trying to get a rise out of Lisa. She would probe for information about Lisa's education, knowing her daughter-in-law had only a two-year degree from a junior college, or ask her about certain poets or composers in an attempt to make Lisa look stupid, which usually worked.

Lisa was up on her Aerosmith and Bono, but didn't know a thing about Bach or Beethoven.

Crossing herself again for good measure, Josephine pondered her daughter's comments, and then tried to reason with her. "I didn't get along good with your father's mother, either, before she died. God rest Carmela's miserable soul. She was a nasty old woman, your grandmother. In fact, Carmela Morelli was so nasty that she made my mother, who's no picnic, look like a saint."

"I heard that!" Grandma Abrizzi shouted from the living room, making Lisa smile.

The elderly woman, who lived with Lisa's parents, was a feisty old gal who said what she thought, shooting straight from the hip and rarely taking any prisoners.

Lisa liked to think she was a lot like her.

"But you didn't marry Alex's mother," Josephine continued. "You married Alex. And I assume, since you went to so much trouble to marry him quickly and outside the sanctity of the church " she kissed the gold cross hanging around her neck "—that you love this husband of yours."

Not about to give her mother any ammunition that the wily woman could use against her, Lisa hedged. "I don't know. All I know is that our marriage was a mistake. As soon as I can afford to hire a lawyer, I'm going to file for divorce."

"That would be a sin, for more than one reason."

"Would you have me live my life and be unhappy? Is that what you want for me?"

"I want all my children to be happy. I want what is best for you, Lisa. You know that. But in my heart I don't believe that divorcing Alex Mackenzie is going to make you happy. In fact, I think it will make you very unhappy and you will come to regret it."

Lisa felt betrayed by what she deemed her mother's lack of support and understanding. "There's no point in discussing this further, Mom. We are not going to agree."

No surprise there! They rarely agreed on anything.

Sighing deeply, Josephine shook her head at her daughter's stubbornness. "So where are you going to get the money to rent an apartment?"

"I intend to find a job to support myself. I've already decided that I don't want any of Alexander's money."

"Have you spoken to Leo about letting you live with him a while longer? You know you can always come home, if he says no."

"I know, Mom, and I appreciate that." *Not!*

"I'm going to talk to Leo this evening when he gets home from work. I'm sure he'll expect me to be gone. He sort of hinted at that this morning. But Francie's going to put in a good word for me today, so maybe he'll be more agreeable by tonight."

"For all of Leo's sins in the eyes of God, he has a good heart."

"Yeah. Let's just hope his generosity and goodness extends to me."

"Living with a gay man is going to be awkward, no? What about his..." Josephine searched for the right word. *"Friends?"*

Lisa shrugged. "That doesn't bother me in the least. To each his own, I say."

"You young people have strange ideas. I don't understand your way of thinking."

Now that was one statement of Josephine Morelli's that she could agree with wholeheartedly.

3

"I REALLY APPRECIATE your letting me move in with you temporarily, Leo," Lisa said, a week after her arrival. "You're a real lifesaver. My own personal fairy godmother."

"Well, that sort of fits, doesn't it?" he replied with a wink. The ability to laugh at himself was one of Leo's greatest gifts.

Lisa dropped the last carton of her belongings onto the living-room floor with a thud, amidst her teddy-bear and Barbie-doll collection, making Leo grit his teeth.

"As long as you understand that it's only temporary, Lisa." The fussy man stared in obvious disgust at the mess she'd already created. "I won't pretend, sweetie, that this was my idea. I invited you to stay here as a favor to Francie, who has assured me that you will be neat as a pin and looking for employment very soon."

Lisa crossed her fingers behind her back. The concept of "neat" wasn't actually part of her vocabulary, so that would take a bit of work on her part. "Absolutely. Neat is my middle name. And I'm heading to the unemployment office first thing in the morning. As soon as I can get my hands on a computer—" Leo looked horrified that she might attempt to use his "—I'm going to post my résumé on one of those job-search sites on the Internet." Of course, she needed to make a résumé first, but there was no need to mention that. Poor Leo seemed traumatized enough as it was.

"Sounds good. I'm sure we'll get along just great. Do you like to dine out?"

Lisa was surprised by the question. "Of course. Who doesn't? Why do you ask?"

"I have a thing about dining out. I love it. And I hate eating alone. Francie used to accompany me. I hope you will, too."

"If you're paying, I'm dining, Leo." Lisa felt as if she'd just died and gone to heaven. Someone actually wanted to pay for her meals; that was more than fine with her. And Leo probably ate at all the best restaurants, which made his request even better.

"And when I don't dine out, I usually order in. I'm not very proficient in the kitchen," he added.

"Don't worry about that. I love to cook. Baking is my specialty." And she was damn good at it, too. Lisa didn't do many things well, but few people could best her when it came to baking. She'd actually thought about taking some classes and trying to bake professionally but, like with most things, Lisa was better at dreaming than doing.

As much as she loved her parents, John and Josephine Morelli had never encouraged either of their daughters to become academic achievers and turn the world on its ear.

For Josephine, getting married and having babies was the greatest accomplishment a woman could strive for, and that's what she was still encouraging her daughters to do.

Fortunately, Francie had always been a go-getter and had made something of herself: she was a bona fide interior designer now.

Lisa had lived up to her parents' expectations of her, which were low to nonexistent, so in that regard she had accomplished something.

Leo's eyes lit up. "Do you know how to make chocolate-chip cookies?"

She grinned from ear to ear. "My chocolate-chip cookies are better than orgasms. You will think Nirvana after the first bite."

"This I gotta see. Make me a list. I'll run down to the market and buy everything you need to make the cookies. What else do you know how to bake?"

Having just discovered Leo's Achilles' heel, Lisa smiled confidently, planning to make the most of it.

LISA LEARNED the following morning that finding a job was not nearly as easy as filling Leo's insatiable craving for sweets.

The red-faced, little pip-squeak behind the counter at the unemployment office had handed Lisa a form, told her to fill it out and return it to him, then wait to be called for an interview.

That had been forty-five minutes ago!

At the rate she was going, she'd be too old and senile

to work and would instead be able to qualify for social-security benefits.

Not that she had anything better to do with her time—unless you counted watching *Wheel of Fortune* reruns on Leo's big-screen TV—but she hated being made to feel like a second-class citizen. She wasn't applying for food stamps; she was trying to find a job so she could support herself, for crying out loud!

"Miss Morelli. Miss Lisa Morelli. Please step up to the counter."

Looking up when her name was announced, Lisa breathed a sigh of relief that her turn had finally come. "Here." She began waving, then stood. "I'm coming," she called out as she made her way toward the counter through the hoard of people waiting in line, openly coveting her good fortune.

At the unemployment office the "you snooze, you lose" rule was firmly in effect.

Mr. Pip-squeak had so many freckles that his face looked like one big red blob. He was looking over her work history and frowning deeply, which didn't bode well for her finding a decent job.

People tended to underestimate her abilities.

"I'm afraid, Miss Morelli, that with your lack of experience, there aren't many jobs available that fit your qualifications."

Lisa couldn't keep the dismay from her face. "But I worked in a bookstore. That should count for something, shouldn't it?"

"That's true. But we have no current listings for that

kind of job. You are, of course, free to apply at the major bookstore chains, if you like. They always need help during the Christmas holidays."

As if she hadn't already done that. Puleeze! And the Christmas holidays were still eleven months away. What was she supposed to do until then, hit the streets with a tin cup?

"What we do have is a job at the Holiday House Motel. It pays minimum wage, but no benefits, I'm afraid."

"Doing what?"

"Cleaning motel rooms, that sort of thing."

She fought the urge to gag. Just what she wanted to do with her life: change sheets that had been soiled from—

Yuck!

"Is that all you have? I must be qualified for something better than that. What about selling cosmetics?" She leaned over the counter. "See how carefully my eyeliner is applied? I'm very good at—"

"Afraid not." Rubbing his chin, he flipped through the thick stack of cards that listed all the current jobs that were available. "There is a job waitressing, but you don't have the experience, I'm afraid."

"The good news is I'm a quick learner. Where's it at?"

"Little Italy. Delisio's Deli."

Lisa's face lit. "I'll take it." She grabbed the card from the startled man's hand and headed toward the door.

"Wait, Miss Morelli! I have to place a call, let them know you're coming. You can't just go there on your own."

"Don't bother. Manny Delisio and I are old friends."
Sort of.

"THAT'S THE FOURTH DISH you've broken in as many days, Lisa. You should be more careful. I'm not made of money, you know."

Old friends, my ass!

Manny's nostrils were flaring, and his new toupee was slightly askew. What Francie ever saw in the guy was beyond Lisa's comprehension. Of course, Manny might have looked good when he was seventeen. He sure as hell didn't now.

It was at the tip of Lisa's tongue to tell Manny that he was the cheapest SOB who had ever walked the face of the earth—or should she say, "slithered?" But then she thought better of it, owing to the fact that she needed this job and the money—not that there was much of it—that went with it.

"Did you get Mrs. Paulie's cheesecake? She's a good customer, don't keep her waiting. She's waving at you. See?"

"I'll get it right now, Manny. And I'll refill her coffee cup, too." Lisa hoped she sounded suitably contrite and efficient, at the same time.

"Good. Now get moving. We haven't got all day."

Mrs. Paulie was her usual charming self when Lisa approached with her order. "About time you brought the coffee and dessert. The other girl who worked here was much more efficient. Are you new? You look new." The old lady peered at her through inch-thick lenses.

"Yes, ma'am. I just started this week."

"Thought so. You're not as good as that other girl."

Deciding not to respond, Lisa had just started to fill the older woman's coffee cup when a four-year-old boy ran by and kicked Lisa behind the right knee, causing her arm to jiggle. The coffee went all over the table, not to mention Mrs. Paulie, who began screaming at the top of her lungs.

"*Shh! Shh!* I'm so sorry, Mrs. Paulie. I'll help you clean up. There's no need to scream."

"Stop, you stupid girl!" She pushed Lisa's hand aside as she attempted to blot up the mess. "Look what you've done. I'm burned! I'm burned!" She jumped up from her chair, causing all the patrons of the delicatessen to look over, including its unhappy, scowling owner who was shooting imaginary bullets at Lisa.

I am so screwed.

"Are you okay, Mrs. Paulie?" Manny asked, rushing over with a handful of clean towels.

The woman glared at him. "Do I look okay? I'm burned, and my dress is ruined."

Lisa thought the dress had been ruined before Mrs. Paulie put it on, it was that ugly. Orange sunflowers. Need she say more?

"Go in the back and stay out of the way, Lisa,"

Manny ordered. "I'll talk to you after I'm done cleaning up your mess."

Without an argument, Lisa hurried to the kitchen, hoping to avoid the glares of the whispering patrons. She found Mr. Tarantino behind the grill, flipping burgers.

"Hey, Mr. T. How's it going?" She liked the older man, even though he smoked and smelled like three-day-old fish. And he liked the fact that she called him "Mr. T." The old TV program *The A-Team* was one of his favorites.

Having overheard Manny's blustering, the grill cook smiled kindly. "Don't worry about Manny, Lisa. He'll get over it. He always does."

"I'm not so sure. He looked pretty mad."

"He and his wife had another fight last night. He's always a shit when that happens. I'm better off not being married, I think."

Lisa smiled. "Thanks, Mr. T. I hope you're right."

"Would you mind watching my burgers for just a sec? I gotta take a leak."

"Sure." Taking the spatula from the man's outstretched hand, Lisa began lifting the burgers to see how cooked they were.

Unfortunately, her action caused the hot pad that was perched precariously close to the edge of the grill to fall onto the hot surface. It ignited immediately.

Flames shot up from the cooktop toward the ceiling before Lisa even realized what was happening. She yelped, trying to remember what to do for a grease fire.

"Flour!" She searched frantically for the canister. "Where the hell is it?" she shouted, becoming more panicked by the second as she watched the flames grow higher and hotter.

"Mr. Tarantino, come quick! We have a problem."

Problem sounded so much better than towering inferno.

But it was Manny who answered her call for help.

He removed the fire extinguisher from the wall, which happened to be located right next to the door leading back into the restaurant, and just a few feet from where Lisa was now standing.

I am so screwed!

"Get back!" he ordered, then began spraying white foam all over the burgers and incinerated hot pad. The fire was put out quickly.

After he was finished, Manny motioned for Lisa to approach the grill area. "You nearly burned down my restaurant."

Lisa swallowed. Her eyes burned, her throat hurt, and now her nerves twitched at the angry look Manny was giving her. "I'm really sorry, Manny. It was an accident. I didn't see the hot pad."

"You see that fire?" He pointed to the grill.

Lisa's forehead wrinkled in confusion. "But the fire's out."

"And so are you. You're fired! Now gather up your things and get out. I can't afford to have you working here. You're not cut out for food service."

"But—" Lisa refused to cry. She wouldn't. Not over a minimum-wage job. But she sure as hell felt like it.

"I'm sorry, Lisa. I like you, but you're a walking disaster."

LISA HAD BEEN CALLED many things in her lifetime, but never a walking disaster. It sounded ominous, undoable.

Accurate?

As she walked back to the apartment, the cold January air seeped beneath her red wool coat, creating a chill clear down to her bones, while a feeling of dread filled her at the prospect of having to tell Francie and Leo that she'd just lost her first job after only three days.

"Crap and a half! Stupid hot pad. Stupid Manny."

Stupid Lisa!

Leo was taking Lisa and Francie out for pizza tonight. Mark was out of town on assignment, and Leo thought that a "girls" night out would be fun, lumping himself into that category, as he so often did. So she knew they'd expect her to regale them about her first week of work.

Francie had been proud of her initiative in finding a job so quickly, and Lisa hated to see the disappointment in her sister's eyes that she knew would be forthcoming, despite the fact that Francie would try to hide it and act supportive.

Like pantyhose a size too small, Francie's support of Lisa was grudgingly given. She wanted Lisa to stand on her own two feet and make something of herself, instead of always screwing up and making excuses.

Lisa was determined not to make any excuses this time.

"IT WASN'T MY FAULT. The damn hot pad fell on the grill. How was I supposed to know that was going to happen? Your friend, Manny, is a real asshole."

Leo and Francie exchanged looks, then Francie said, "Manny's not an asshole, just short-tempered and not very patient. And you did almost burn down his deli."

"Yeah, and I would have been pissed about that," Leo said, sipping his beer. "I happen to love his Reubens and meatball subs. I'm getting hungry just thinking about them."

"How can you be hungry when you're stuffing your face with pizza?" Lisa reached for another slice of the mushroom-and-sausage pie, then said, "I'll check the paper in the morning to see if there are any other jobs listed."

She was not going to work at that disgusting motel. Lisa had promised herself that she was better than that. Dried sperm on dirty sheets was just not her thing.

"I'm sure you'll be able to find something, Lisa," Francie said with a smile of encouragement. "You're smart and clever. I bet there are lots of jobs you can do."

"Thanks. Unfortunately, the guy at the unemployment office doesn't share your opinion. He pretty much indicated that I sucked."

"I have a friend who has a dog-walking business,"

Leo said. "I'll give Warren a call and see if he needs any help."

Lisa brightened. "I love dogs! That would be great. Thanks, Leo!"

"So have you heard from your husband?" Lisa's new roommate wanted to know, leaning forward. "You haven't said much about him lately."

"Leo..." Francie cautioned with a shake of her head.

"What? I'm Lisa's landlord. I have a right to know. Plus, I like to gossip."

Sighing, Lisa shook her head. "No. Alex hasn't called or made contact." That wasn't quite true. There'd been a few hang ups on Leo's answering machine, and Lisa wondered if those might have been Alex trying to reach her. Though she had no idea how he would know where she was. She hadn't left a forwarding address, and she doubted if he cared, at any rate.

"Well, I'm sure he'll contact you soon, Lisa. Just give him time. You wounded Alex's ego. No doubt he's biding his time and licking his wounds."

"His wounds? I'm the one who got trashed, remember?"

Francie patted her sister's hand. "Don't get upset. You know better than anyone how weird men can be."

THE PERFECT EXAMPLE of that male weirdness was sitting over in the dark corner of the restaurant at that moment, spying on Lisa, Francie and Leo.

Alex had been following Lisa around the last few

days, in the hope of talking to her. He'd tried calling
Leo's apartment a few times after discovering, quite by
accident—he'd been on his way to Francie's apartment
and had spotted Lisa entering the apartment across the
hall—where she'd been living. But he hadn't had the
guts to leave a message, knowing it was extremely un-
likely that she would return his phone call.

Having decided that an up-close and personal confrontation was the only way he was going to get Lisa to
talk to him, Alex had been following her until the opportunity presented itself.

So far, it hadn't.

She was either with her family and friends, applying
for jobs, burning down buildings, or hiding out.

He, too, had been looking for work, though only
halfheartedly. Alex had finally decided that rather than
work for someone else as a mortgage banker, he would
open up his own firm.

He'd spent the last few days—when he wasn't spying on Lisa, that is—researching locations for his business and talking to some of the contacts he'd made
over the years in the banking industry.

Alex was determined to become the kind of man that
his wife wanted.

Seeing Lisa, even from a distance, made his heart
ache. And damn, but she looked good. Tonight she was
wearing a tight black-leather skirt and fuzzy red
sweater—the one he had given her for Christmas—and
she looked hot.

He sipped his beer, feeling his pants tighten. Lisa

had always had the power to affect him this way, and she probably always would.

She and her companions were laughing, and the sound of his wife's high-pitched giggle made Alex smile. He hadn't heard her laugh like that in ages and knew he was to blame.

Why hadn't he recognized her unhappiness and growing dissatisfaction with his family? Why had he tried to convince her to go along with his parents' wishes, to placate them, as he always had?

He'd known from the first moment he'd met her that Lisa was a free spirit. It was what had drawn him to her. She was so totally different from the other women he had dated. So why then had he tried to stifle that in her? Why had he tried to make her into something she wasn't?

Fear? Ignorance? An unwillingness to rock the boat? All of the above?

"Oh, Lisa, I'm so damn sorry."

Suddenly, she turned and looked in his direction, as if she could hear him calling her name. But he knew, of course, that she couldn't. He'd picked the table behind the slatted partition, so he could observe her, not the other way around.

He would make his move when the time was right. But that wasn't now, Alex's gut told him. Lisa needed a bit more time to get over her anger. But a few romantic gestures wouldn't be a bad idea. And first thing tomorrow he'd put his plan into motion.

4

TWO DAYS AFTER HER DINNER with Francie and Leo, Lisa began walking dogs to earn a living.

Or rather, the dogs walked her.

She had the morning shift and had to be at her various destinations beginning at 6:00 a.m., a terrible time for Lisa, who was not a morning person and did not function well until she had at least three cups of Starbucks' French Roast.

"Stop it, Blossom!" Lisa ordered the Boston terrier, who had a nasty habit of taking a dump in the middle of the sidewalk. She'd been given a handful—no pun intended—of plastic bags to scoop up the poop by Leo's friend Warren, owner of the dog-walking business. As if she was really going to do something that disgusting. Picking up dog poop ranked right up there with sperm-laden bed sheets, in her opinion.

"Not in my lifetime!" she told the dog, who merely wagged what passed for a tail.

Rather than pick up the offending leavings, Lisa preferred to stroll casually up to them and nudge the piles out of the way with her foot. Fortunately, she wore galoshes for this nasty chore, which helped only a little.

Shit was, after all...shitty.

Carting a now lighter Blossom up the stairs to her owner's town house, Lisa unlocked the door with the key she'd been given and stuck the poor dog in her portable kennel.

"Sorry, Blossom love, but don't blame me," she said when the dog gazed at her forlornly and whined. "It's your mean, nasty parents' fault, not mine. I would never leave you locked up all day. Your owners should be shot."

Having said that, Lisa looked up to find said "mean, nasty parent" of the male variety, staring furiously at her, mouth opening and closing like a floundering fish.

Apparently, Mr. Bowles had left his briefcase behind and had returned to his apartment to fetch it.

I am so screwed!

"Warren shall hear about this, young woman."

Thus ended Lisa's dog-walking career.

Warren heard about it and had canned her that same evening. By the next day Lisa was poring over the want ads again, wondering how she was going to break the news to Leo, who had previously dated Warren and wanted to leave a good impression.

"Well, Leo can just get over it," Lisa said to herself. "Warren was a putz, anyway." Of course, Warren was a working putz, whereas Lisa was of the nonworking variety.

Running her pencil down the long columns of employment ads, Lisa began rejecting as she went: waitress—too stressful, movie cashier—too boring, nursing-home attendant—too depressing.

She'd been around her Grandma Abruzzi enough to know that many older people had personality quirks, to put it mildly.

No thank you!

Pausing on one provocative header, which indicated that qualified applicants could make shit-loads of money—only they referred to it as "substantial income"—she considered the ad.

Erotic dancer wanted. Experience preferred but not necessary. Nights and weekends required. Costumes supplied.

All she had to do was dance in a nightclub...in front of hundreds of leering men...half naked.

"Piece of cake. I walk around this apartment in my bra and panties all the time and Leo isn't fazed by it one bit."

Owing to the fact that Leo was gay, of course.

"I have a good body, not too much cellulite that would make someone want to vomit. I can dance in a skimpy costume and make lots of money."

How hard could that be?

And a job in the entertainment industry was prestigious. Everyone she knew—well, maybe not Francie, and okay, maybe not her mother—was sure to be impressed.

Wasn't this how that famous stripper Gypsy Rose Lee got her start? And Gypsy went on to write books and had a play named after her. Not bad for a woman who took her clothes off for a living and cavorted around in the buff.

Calling the phone number listed in the ad before she

could chicken out, Lisa made an appointment the following afternoon with someone named Spike.

Gulp!

"I CAN'T BELIEVE I let you talk me into going nightclubbing with you tonight, Bill," Alex said, taking a sip of his beer and trying to make himself heard over the shouts and whistles of the mostly male patrons of The Playful Kitten Club. "This place is a dive. How'd you find it?" The kittens looked more like hellcats, and that was in dim light.

Bill laughed. "Some of the guys from my firm come here to unwind after work. They told me about it. I thought it would be just the ticket to get your mind off your wife. You've been pissing and moaning about her for days on end. We could both use a break. And who knows, you might get lucky. Some of the women they've got dancing here are pretty hot."

Alex hadn't noticed. He wasn't interested in any woman, except Lisa. "I'm not looking for a one-night stand, Bill. I'm married, remember?"

"Sounds like a formality to me, buddy. Your wife deserted you. You've got grounds for divorce. And if you're smart, you'll file before she beats you to it. That way, she might not take you for everything you're worth."

Bill glanced up at the stage and whistled. "Man! Look at that! She must be new. I've never seen her here before."

"Not interested," Alex said, ordering another beer

from the waitress and trying to ignore Bill's running commentary.

"She's got a killer body and long black hair that a man could run his hands through. Man, but wouldn't I like a taste of that. The woman's a goddess."

Bill's effusive praise finally pricked Alex's curiosity, and he turned in his seat, staring up at the stage. His mouth dropped open and the beer mug he'd been holding fell to the floor with a crash, spilling the contents everywhere, but he didn't notice, or care.

The sight of his wife dancing up on stage in front of a dozen or more leering men, dressed in nothing but a G-string and sequined bra, had his blood boiling over, filling him with a jealous, killing rage, the likes of which he'd never known before.

"I told you she was hot."

Alex grabbed Bill's arm. "Shut up, you ass! That's Lisa. That's my wife, you're talking about."

Bill's eyes widened. "No shit! No wonder you want her back. She is one good-looking woman, if you don't mind my saying so."

"I do mind. Come on. We've got to leave before she sees me," Alex said, tugging his friend's arm. "I don't want her to know I'm here in Philadelphia."

"Why the hell not? I thought you came here to get your wife back. How can you do that if you don't talk to her and let her know how sorry you are about everything?"

"Lisa will think I'm spying on her, if she sees me."

Alex *had* been spying on Lisa, but usually only during the day, figuring her nights had been spent at Leo's or Francie's apartment, not at some exotic-dance club.

Never in a million years would he have suspected Lisa of doing something so totally outlandish. His wife might have a wild streak, but she was also sensible. Or so he'd thought.

Dancing naked in front of men did not constitute sensible behavior.

"Well, you are. You've been following the woman around for days like frigging Sherlock Holmes. And I refuse to play Dr. Watson."

Once outside the bar, Alex released his hold on Bill and said, "Look, I know this sounds crazy, but I know my wife. Or I think I do. I've got to do this my way, in my own time. Do you understand?"

The night air was cold, and the attorney turned the collar of his suit jacket up. "Hell, no, I don't understand. But it's your life, so I'm not going to interfere more than I have already. I just hope to hell you know what you're doing."

"Me, too," Alex said in a voice that held zero confidence.

LISA HAD BEEN WORKING at the Playful Kitten Club for almost a week and had been pulling in some very good tips. She'd only had to punch out one overzealous customer, who'd tried to shove more than a twenty-dollar bill into her G-string.

All in all, it had been pretty decent. The women she worked with seemed nice—some were college students, others single mothers trying to make ends meet. It wasn't a job anyone particularly relished doing, but if you needed money, it was the means to an end.

Lisa felt fortunate that she hadn't seen anyone she knew at the nightclub. The heavy makeup she wore would probably keep most people, even friends, from recognizing her. At least, she hoped so. After observing the clientele, and the general seediness of the club, she'd decided that none of her friends would consider what she was doing to earn a living in show biz.

A perverse part of Lisa wished that Alex could see her now, dancing and being the object of so much male adoration. He might become jealous, realize what he had given up.

Not that she cared!

Much.

The awful truth was, she missed Alex. They'd shared so many wonderful moments during their brief marriage—romantic interludes on the beach, intimate conversations about growing up with such diverse family backgrounds.

But most of all, they'd had fun.

And great sex!

Lisa wasn't the type of woman who adjusted well to celibacy. She liked sex, and wasn't afraid to admit it. She owned a vibrator, and wasn't afraid to admit that, either. Of course, she hadn't used it since before her marriage to Alex. There'd been no need, not with her virile, sexy husband to take care of matters for her.

But unfortunately things had changed. She made a mental note to check her batteries.

Sighing, she wrapped her terry robe more tightly around her and strolled into the kitchen to see what delights Leo had in his freezer.

She didn't have to work tonight, and ice cream was a definite cure-all for loneliness and depression. She'd eaten her fair share of it in the past few weeks.

Lisa had just removed a large tub of Baskin-Robbins Pralines and Cream and placed it on the kitchen counter when the phone rang. It was Francie.

"I was hoping you were up. I never know what time to call, what with your dog-walking in the morning and your job at the movie theater at night."

Lisa's face grew hot. "I'm off tonight." She felt guilty that she hadn't confided in Francie and Leo about her new job, or the fact that she'd been fired from the old one. But she knew her sister would disapprove and be worried for her, so she'd said nothing.

Suddenly, the doorbell rang, and Lisa wondered who was visiting so late. "Hold on, France. Someone's at the door."

"Be sure to see who it is first before you open it."

"Yes, Mother."

Lisa opened the door to find a florist deliveryman standing there. "Lisa Mackenzie," he said, holding out the large bouquet.

With her heart beating fast, Lisa took the flowers, thanked the young man and then headed back to the kitchen, setting them on the counter, where she could see them.

Since arriving back in Philadelphia, she hadn't been using her married name, so the flowers could have only come from one person. Taking the card from the holder, she discovered she was right.

I Miss You! Love, Alex.

Alex had sent flowers! But why? And why now, after so many days had passed? His card said he missed her. So why hadn't he tried to contact her before?

Not that she would have spoken to him.

But still...

Inhaling the glorious scent of roses, Lisa made an instant decision not to tell her sister about them. "I'm back."

"Who was it?"

"Just someone selling something I didn't want."

"I hate that. What's wrong? You sound tired."

"Nothing. Well, I am kind of tired."

"I won't keep you. I was just wondering if you'd like to come for dinner tomorrow evening. Mark and I are having a few friends in, and I thought it would be nice if you could come, sort of be my cheerleader. I'm a bit nervous."

The invitation was met by silence.

"Lisa? Lisa! Are you all right?"

"I can't. I have to work."

"But can't you call in sick or something? It's Saturday night."

Lisa knew she would make gobs of money at the

club on a Saturday night, it being the busiest night of the week, and she couldn't afford to take the time off, especially after missing tonight, which was the second busiest night.

"Now who's being irresponsible? I have to work, remember? Leo isn't letting me stay here for free, you know. My share of the rent will be due soon."

Francie sighed loudly. "I guess you're right. I'm just disappointed since this is my first official dinner party as Mrs. Mark Fielding, and I wanted you to be there."

"I would have loved to come, you know that. But you'll do fine without me, France. I'm sure Leo will be happy to help out. And Mom, if you want her."

"*Puhleeze!* Josephine would take over and insist on doing everything. It's Ma's way. I'm not inviting our parents, Lisa. Do you think that's wrong of me?"

"No, of course not! Don't be ridiculous. Children should not have to socialize with their parents, unless they have to borrow money, or their parents are on life support."

Francie laughed. "I knew I could count on you to talk some sense into me."

"It's usually the other way around."

"Don't sell yourself short, Lisa. Look at how you've turned things around. You're working two jobs, sharing an apartment and paying rent, making the best of a bad situation. I'm really proud of you."

Lisa's eyes filled with tears and a lump lodged in her throat. "Thanks. I gotta go, okay? I've got something on the stove." It was a lie, but Lisa wasn't about to admit to her older sister that Francie's compliments and faith in her was making her cry. Lisa didn't deserve the praise, not under the present circumstances, at any rate.

She was working as an exotic dancer. Her marriage was on the rocks. And her life sucked majorly!

"I KNEW YOU WOULD LIKE the flowers, love. The softness of the petals, so dewy and moist, reminded me of you."

"Alex, Alex, we shouldn't. I'm too upset and angry with you," Lisa moaned when Alex's hand moved to touch her breast and toy with her nipples.

"You know you want me. Isn't that why you invited me to come here tonight, so we could make love?" He kissed her then, stealing her breath and whatever sense she had left to think rational thoughts.

What she was doing was definitely not rational.

"I do want you, Alex. I've always wanted you. But this is wrong. We shouldn't be together like this, not after everything—"

"Ssh!" His hand moved up her nightgown to rest on the juncture of her thighs. "I can make you feel good. Remember how it always is between us?"

"Yes!" she said breathlessly. "Yes! Yes!"

Her legs opened and his fingers moved to caress her aching bud. "Let yourself go, Lisa. You know you want to. Don't hold anything back."

But some part of her resisted. "I can't. I can't."

"Yes, you can." His lips were persuasive as he kissed her protests away, his tongue plunging in, his clever

fingers moving purposefully over the center of her being.

"Oh, Alex! Oh, oh..."

"Oh shit!"

Lisa awoke with a start to find herself in bed, and
quite alone. Sweat beaded her forehead. She'd been so
damn close to, to... If it had only been a damn dream,
then why in hell did she have to wake up now? Just a
few more seconds and—

"Damn you, Alex!"

Tears of frustration streamed down her face as she
inhaled the sweet scent of the flowers he'd sent to her,
which she'd moved into the bedroom with her.

Picking up the vase from the nightstand, she heaved
it across the room where it crashed against the wall in
a million pieces, sort of like her heart.

"I can't do anything right."

And that included masturbation, apparently.

"Shit! Shit! Shit!"

Shutting off the lamp, she shut her eyes and forced
herself to think of the most hateful and unpleasant
thing she could.

Unfortunately, that was Alex.

TEN DAYS AFTER Lisa had started working at the club,
the shit hit the fan.

Leo had talked Francie into going to a new bar he'd
heard about, The Playful Kitten, for some drinks and a
few laughs. With Mark out of town again, Francie had
agreed and they were now seated at a table in front of

the stage, surrounded by hoards of enthusiastic male customers, waiting for the next act to appear.

When Lisa, dressed in a short apron and not much else, strutted on stage to the Donna Summer song, "She Works Hard for the Money," Francie gasped in shock, then screamed much louder than the patrons. She would have fallen off her chair, if Leo hadn't been there to steady her.

"Oh my God! It's Lisa. She's naked!"

"Ain't it great?" the big oaf standing behind her shouted, in between whistles and loud clapping.

"Shut up! It's not great. It's disgusting!"

His expression was one of disbelief. "You're nuts, lady! What are you, one of those Carrie Nationwide women, or something?"

Francie was about to answer with a rude comment when Leo shook his head and said to the guy, "My friend's had too much to drink. I'm taking her home."

"Good. We don't need no prudes around here, spoiling all the fun. Jesus, lady, you should get a job in vice."

"You pervert!" Francie retorted, rising from her chair, a murderous gleam in her eye. "You should be ashamed of yourself. You're practically old enough to be her father. If my husband was here, he'd show—"

"Come on, Francie," Leo urged, clasping her arm and tugging. "We're leaving."

She shrugged him off. "I'm not going home, Leo. I need to put a stop to this."

"You're Lisa's sister, not her keeper, or her mother," he reminded her.

Francie paled. "My God! If my mother saw Lisa like this she'd have that heart attack she's always talking about." Josephine threatened heart failure at least once a week.

"Let's go."

"But—"

"Lisa will be home soon. We'll talk to her then."

"But—"

"But nothing. We're going home. Now!"

LISA WAS SURPRISED to find Leo up and Francie at the apartment when she returned home from work, and wondered how she was going to explain the heavy makeup she still wore. She decided, if asked, that she would tell them it was *Rocky Horror Picture Show* night at the movie theater.

"You guys having a party or something? It's kinda late to be up chatting, isn't it?" Lisa removed her coat and joined them in the living room, despite the fact she was dog tired. Her feet hurt, her back ached and even her mouth was numb from smiling so much.

Gazing at her sister, Lisa noted that Francie had been crying. Her nose was red—a dead giveaway. Moving to sit on the sofa beside her, she asked, "Is something wrong, France? Is it Mark?"

Francie shook her head. "No, it's not Mark. It's you, Lisa."

"Me?" Lisa's eyes widened. What on earth was

Francie talking about? "But I'm perfectly fine, as you can see."

"We saw more than we wanted to see tonight, Lisa, that's for damn sure. Leo and I visited The Playful Kitten Club and guess who we saw dancing up on stage? It was traumatic, to say the least."

Consumed by guilt and embarrassment, Lisa tried to brazen it out, nevertheless. "Oh, come on. I'm not that bad." She turned to Leo and smiled a fake smile, not unlike the ones she used to entertain her customers. "Didn't you think I was pretty good, Leo? I've got natural rhythm, you've got to admit that."

Leo nodded. "You were great, sweetie. We heard many admiring comments from the male customers."

"Shut up, Leo! Don't feed her ego." Francie chastised her former roommate, then said to her sister, "You've got to quit that job. It's dangerous for you to be working there. That place is filled with nothing but voyeurs and perverts."

Lisa sighed. "I knew you would disapprove, which is why I didn't tell you what I was doing to earn a living, France."

"I take it the dog-walking thing didn't work out," Leo said.

"Warren fired me." She explained the situation with Blossom's parent. "I wasn't really enamored of the job, anyway. I mean, the dogs were cute and all, but I hated picking up the crap."

"You'd rather dance naked in front of strange men than pick up dog poop? *Unfriggingbelievable*." Francie shook her head. "What if Mom and Dad had seen you? Or Alex? Did you ever think of that?"

"I'm a grown woman, Francie. I don't need a lecture, especially from you. I'm not selling myself. I'm just dancing. It's a perfectly respectable job, much better than working as a hotel maid and coming into contact with various bodily fluids, I might add."

"I want you to quit, Lisa."

"I can't quit. I need the money. And it's not going to be a career. I'm only doing it temporarily, until I can save enough money to get a place of my own. I'm sure Leo is anxious to get rid of me."

Leo's silence on the subject was rather telling, until Francie kicked him in the leg.

"Don't be silly. You're welcome to stay here as long as you like," he added quickly, and Lisa almost smiled at the poor man, wondering how his sanity survived dealing with the Morelli sisters.

"Thanks, Leo, but I'm hoping it won't be for too much longer."

"Leo and I have been talking since we got home, Lisa. We've come up with an idea that we thought might solve your problem."

"You haven't found me a wealthy man to marry, have you? Because...well, I've already had one of those."

Lisa wondered again what Alex's motives were in pursuing her. She refused to believe that he loved her, not after the awful way he had allowed his parents to treat her. If that was love, she wanted no part of it.

Shaking her head, Francie finally smiled. "We'd like you to come to work for Designing Women. You'd be a gofer at first, running errands, picking up materials and delivering them. But if you work hard and prove yourself, you can work into a position as a designer."

"With your theatrical ability, Lisa, you'd be a natural," Leo added, smiling enthusiastically as he warmed to the idea.

"And you've agreed to this, Leo?" Lisa shook her head, confusion marring her features. "You've only just opened for business. How can you afford to hire me?"

"Sweetie, money has never been a problem for me. I've got tons of it. And if a job will get you out of that awful club, then I'm happy to hire you."

Tears filled Lisa's eyes. "You're very sweet. You know that, don't you?"

"Of course, I know that. For years, women have been wishing I were straight. Alas, I've had to disappoint them. As beautiful and sexy as you looked up on that stage tonight, it didn't do a thing for me."

Lisa laughed. "You know, Leo, you shouldn't be saying stuff like that. I'm a woman who likes a challenge. I just might be tempted to turn you to the dark side."

"Well, if you're a woman who likes a challenge," Francie interrupted, "then come to work with us at Designing Women. Leo's an excellent teacher, we have a new office that he has decorated exquisitely, and I promise that you'll learn a lot. I certainly have in the short time I've been working there."

Lisa mentally calculated the pros and cons of the offer. She knew the money wouldn't be as good as what she was making at the club, but it would give her an opportunity to learn a real profession and work with two people she adored. It would also keep peace in the family, and her feet wouldn't hurt any longer!

"All right, I'll do it."

5

DONNING HER COAT, Lisa was about to head out of the apartment to her first day of work at Designing Women when the doorbell rang.

Damn! She checked her watch, knowing she couldn't afford to be late on her very first day. She hadn't given two weeks notice at the club, so if Leo fired her, she'd be up shit creek without the proverbial paddle.

"Oh hell! Why now?" She wasn't a morning person and had overslept again.

No surprise there!

Tempted not to answer, she reconsidered, just in case it was someone or something for Leo. It was his apartment, after all, and she didn't want to be rude.

Leo had a lot of friends. Hell, he had more friends than Bette Midler could sing about.

Opening the door, Lisa stood there in shock and disbelief, staring at the handsome visage that was her husband and ignoring the way her traitorous heart lurched.

Like her he was dressed casually—only Lisa wore blue jeans and a T-shirt, while Alex was dressed in neatly pressed khakis, the crease just so, and a lightly starched blue shirt that brought out the color of his eyes. He wouldn't have been caught dead in jeans. His mama would never have approved, she thought meanly.

"Hello, Lisa."

She fought her delight at seeing him, pushing aside the memories of her perverted dream, and asked in a brusque manner, "What are you doing here?"

"I've missed you, love. We need to talk."

"I don't have time to talk," she replied, trying to ignore the endearment and keep her emotions in check. "I'm late for work."

Alex's lips formed a thin slash. "Since when do nightclubs open this early?"

Her eyes narrowed. "Have you been spying on me?" For days she'd had the creepy sensation that someone was watching her. But, of course, she'd brushed it off as her vivid imagination. Now it seemed she wasn't so crazy, after all. Alex had been keeping tabs on her. And while one part of her liked that idea, because it meant he still cared, the other part—her feminist part—was furious.

"I'm staying with a friend from college, Bill Connors. He insisted we go nightclubbing the other night, and we ended up at The Playful Kitten Club."

Lisa knew she paled slightly, but otherwise didn't respond.

"It was quite an illuminating evening I can assure you. Not many husbands get to watch their wives cavort half-naked on stage in front of a roomful of leering men. Why did you behave so—?"

"Wantonly?" she supplied with a naughty smile, which lasted only a brief second, but still had the power to deepen his scowl. "First of all, the fact that I'm still your wife is a mere technicality. I don't have the money to hire a lawyer just yet, but when I do, that'll be it. We'll be history. And what I do with my life in the meantime is none of your damn business. We're separated, in case you haven't noticed."

"You're my wife!" he insisted. "I never agreed to a separation."

"That's your problem, not mine. Now please step out of my way. I have to leave for work."

"This isn't over yet, Lisa."

"Oh, really? Well, it certainly seems over. And you can quit sending me flowers with love notes attached, because if you really loved me, Alexander Mackenzie, you would have tried to contact me long before now. I could have been dead, for all you cared."

Okay, so they hadn't been separated for even a month yet, but still...

Wincing at the hurt in her voice, Alex reached for Lisa, but she stepped back just in time. "I thought I was being kind by giving you time to get over your anger. I was frantic with worry after you disappeared. You left no note, no explanation as to where you had gone or what I had done."

"*Ha!* You didn't even try to call, that's how much you cared." And for Alex not to know what he had done was ludicrous, laughable, an out-and-out lie.

"I didn't know where you were. And I did call, several times. I just didn't leave a message."

"So that was you? And you had to have been spying on me to know where I lived."

"I wasn't spying. Well, not exactly. I came across that information quite by accident."

"What did you do, pay a private investigator to locate me, or threaten my mother for the information?" Josephine would have been only too happy to spill the beans. The Terminator was a till-death-do-us-part kind of woman.

"No, nothing that dramatic. I paid a visit to your sister's apartment. Francie wasn't home, but while I was there I happened to see you enter Leo's place, and I put two and two together."

"Well, now you know. Leo and I are living together, and we're very happy. In fact, I've never been happier."

His amused smile said he didn't believe a word she was saying. "Leo is gay."

"*Hmph!* That's how much you know. He went straight as an arrow for me. In fact, I'm working for him at Designing Women. I'm going to become an interior designer. Leo thinks I have oodles of talent." She raised an eyebrow meaningfully. "And not just in design."

Alex shook his head. "If that man is straight, then I'm the frigging king of England."

"Don't you mean *queen*? Excuse me," Lisa said, pushing Alex out of the way as she exited the apartment, shutting the door behind her. "I have to go. It's been lovely talking with you, Alex. Have a nice life."

"You are, without a doubt, the most stubborn, irrational woman on the face of this earth."

Pausing, Lisa turned back. "We can't all be sweetness and light, like your mama. Now can we, Alex?"

Confusion creased his eyebrows. "My mother? What does she have to do with this?"

Oh, puhleeze! Was he really that dense?

Well, he was a man.

"Everything, you dolt. Everything."

WATCHING LISA WALK AWAY, Alex felt a multitude of emotions: Love. He was more in love with his wife than ever. She was beautiful, stubborn, exasperating—and he was crazy about her. Guilt, as his worst suspicions had just been confirmed. It had been his parents' treatment of Lisa that had caused her to bolt. And he was to blame. He should have stepped in, taken her side, done what any good husband would have done to protect the woman he loved. And hope. He'd do everything in his power to win her back.

Why was I so stupid?

"Dammit!"

His parents were snobbish, foolish people, but they weren't monsters. He was positive they had acted out of love for him. But there was no denying that their behavior toward Lisa had been mean-spirited.

At first, she had tried to please them, but it was hard to satisfy Miriam and Rupert Mackenzie. They lived by their own rules and value system, and they weren't about to change now.

Age did that to people. Made them rigid and unbending in their beliefs.

Lisa had confessed that she'd had similar problems with her parents. They'd never accepted her for who she was and were always trying to change her, make her conform to what they considered normal behavior. And then she had received the exact same treatment from his mother and father.

Alex sighed, tunneling frustrated fingers through his hair and wishing he'd had this insight several months ago.

It had taken this disaster with Lisa for Alex to finally realize that though his parents had meant well, in their own self-serving way, it was time for him to stand on his own two feet and make his own decisions.

Living up to his father's expectations had been the driving force behind many of the choices Alex had made in his life, but not anymore. He was determined to become his own man.

And it was about damn time!

Resigning from his father's firm had been an important first step. Now he was putting his plan into motion. He'd already spoken to several bankers and had another appointment with Citicorp today. He'd found a good downtown location and hoped to rent it, as soon as he could float the loan he needed.

Alex had his grandmother's inheritance, but that money wasn't enough to fund this venture. Investors

were definitely the best way to go, and he had several
more interested individuals to talk to.

But first, he needed to talk to Josephine Morelli.

Based on what Lisa had told him previously, her
mother was pleased that she'd finally gotten married
and settled down. Alex figured the older woman
couldn't be happy about his and Lisa's estrangement
and might be willing to help him convince his stubborn
wife to reconcile.

It was worth a shot, anyway.

"YOU'RE LATE! And I can tell you right now that Leo is
a stickler about things like that. So if you want to keep
this job, in the future you'd better show up on time."

Lisa nodded at her sister, hanging her coat on the
brass rack in Francie's office. "I know. I'm sorry. But I
have a really good excuse. Alex came by to see me this
morning, just as I was leaving for work."

"You're kidding!" Francie's eyes were huge as she
handed Lisa a cup of coffee, then patted the space next
to her on the blue-suede sofa. "Tell me everything.
Were you happy to see him? Did he apologize?
Where's he been all this time?"

Sipping the hot coffee, Lisa attempted to push Alex's
disturbing image out of her mind; she barely succeeded. "He's been here in Philadelphia, staying with
an old college buddy or so he tells me. And he's been
spying on me. Alex knew about my job at the nightclub. In fact, he saw me perform."

Francie smiled. "How romantic, about the spying I mean. It shows that Alex really cares about you, Lisa."

"It shows that he's too nosy for his own good. I told him to knock it off, and I also told him to quit sending me flowers." Realizing she'd slipped, Lisa slapped a hand over her mouth.

"Alex sent you flowers? You never told me."

"It was the night we were on the phone and the doorbell rang. Remember? And I didn't tell you because I knew you'd get all excited and read stuff into it that didn't belong."

"He loves you. I knew it. How can you deny that?"

"I just do. Alex is probably more interested in keeping up appearances, like his parents. Most likely it didn't go over well at the club when they found out his wife had left him."

"Oh, Lisa, you don't really believe that, do you?"

Lisa shrugged. "I don't know what to believe anymore." And that was the absolute truth. She'd had so many conflicting emotions since seeing Alex this morning: love, hate, disappointment...love.

Dammit!

"What I do know is that if I don't get started working, Leo is going to fire me. And I refuse to be fired on my first day again. It's too humiliating. I don't think my ego—what's left of it, anyway—could take another shot."

Smiling in understanding, Francie patted her sister's hand. "I think having you around is going to be much more entertaining than watching a soap opera. I know we're going to have fun working together."

Lisa thought so, too. "So what's my first assignment? And where's Leo?"

"Leo drove to New York City to pick up fabric for a customer."

"But I thought that was my job." Lisa couldn't keep the disappointment out of her voice. She'd been looking forward to going to New York and had planned to get some shopping in, once her work was completed, and maybe lunch at a fancy restaurant now that she was gainfully employed again.

"It is. But Leo's nervous about this new customer. Mrs. Wallace is very picky and persnickety, and he didn't want anything to go wrong. Not that he thought it would," Francie added quickly, "if you'd done the pickup."

"I hope not, because I really want to do a good job here. I plan to work very hard and make a new career for myself." Although Lisa hadn't quite convinced herself that interior design was her calling. But she was willing to give it a try.

"That's good. And since you're so determined to get to work, you can start by hauling some of these fabric swatches into the showroom. I have an appointment with the ever delightful—Not!—Mrs. Melbourne, who's changed her mind about the fabric she picked out over six weeks ago for her living-room drapes.

"Of course, this is only the third time she's changed her mind. I had to call and cancel the last two orders, which thrilled my supplier to no end, but the customer comes first, right?"

Lisa gazed at her sister as if she'd lost her mind. "Are you serious? I'd have told the old bat to shove it. Once somebody picks out fabrics, they should have to stick with them."

Francie grinned. "That is why you're not working with clients just yet, Lisa. First, we need to give you a crash course in the care and nurturing of customers."

"I should have stuck with dogs. At least they don't talk back."

"No, but apparently their angry owners do."

"Okay, okay, I get the picture. I'll just shut up and do my job."

"Good." Francie picked a sheet of paper up off her desk and handed it to Lisa. "Here's a list of the fabric samples I need. Mrs. Melbourne will be here in twenty minutes, so you'd better get started."

Dismayed, Lisa's eyes widened. "Hell, this could take the rest of the day," she said, staring at the large number of swatches she had to pull.

"Yes, it could. But it's only going to take you twenty minutes, right?"

Heaving a sigh, Lisa wondered why gainful employment had to be part of her vocabulary. "Right."

JOSEPHINE MORELLI answered the door on the third knock, and by the huge smile on her face, Alex knew Lisa's mother was happy to see him. In fact, she looked as if she'd been expecting him, and her next words confirmed it.

"I've been wondering when you were going to show up, Alexander Mackenzie. I'm glad you decided to get your head on straight. Women like my daughter don't come along every day. I hope you know that."

"May I come in, Mrs. Morelli? I'd like to talk to you about Lisa."

The older woman, looking a little bit like a tattered American flag in faded blue polyester pants, a red sweater and a white apron, led Alex into the kitchen and seated him at the table, then busied herself at the stove.

Setting a plate of pasta and a glass of wine before him, she said, "It's lunchtime. We'll eat, and then we'll talk. Conversation can sometimes ruin a good lunch, and my stomach's not what it used to be. I think it's my heart, but don't tell my girls. I wouldn't want them to worry."

Privy to the heart-attack hypochondria, Alex just nodded. He had already eaten a hamburger before coming over, but he knew it would be a major mistake to offend Lisa's mother, who was offering him hospitality, if not heartburn. "Thanks! It looks delicious. I love linguini."

They ate in silence for several minutes, then Josephine looked up, fork poised in midair, and said, "What happened between you and my daughter?" apparently willing to risk indigestion rather than wait any longer to get all the gory details.

Alex's eyebrows shot up. "You mean, Lisa hasn't told you?" He figured his wife had told everyone every little secret about their marriage.

"I want to hear your version of the story. Sometimes a woman can be a bit too emotional."

Nodding, he heaved a deep sigh. "It was a mistake moving in with my parents. We should have stayed in Philadelphia and made a life on our own, I realize that now. My parents weren't welcoming to Lisa. I thought they'd come around eventually, but they didn't."

"What's wrong with them, that they don't like my daughter? I admit, Lisa has her ways, but she's a good girl and she was brought up properly with good manners. My husband and I saw to that."

"There's nothing wrong with Lisa. She's wonderful. It's my parents. They're wealthy and...well, they're snobs. They go for appearances and pedigrees."

Josephine's eyes widened. "Like dogs?" She cursed softly under her breath, and Alex was grateful he didn't speak Italian.

"They didn't take the time to get to know Lisa, as I do. If they had, they would have loved and treated her much differently."

"Why didn't you stand up for your wife? Are you a mama's boy, like my daughter says? Not that there's anything wrong with that. A boy should show respect to his mother. But still... It's in the Bible."

Alex smiled. "You could say that. My mother has doted on me my entire life. I was an only child because she couldn't have more children."

"Children are a gift from God."

"I should have stood up to my parents when they began attacking Lisa, but I thought they'd relent. I guess I didn't realize the extent of their nastiness. Though I know that's no excuse."

Sipping her wine thoughtfully, Josephine finally asked, "And now what do you intend to do?"

Full to bursting, Alex set down his fork. "That's why I've come to you, Mrs. Morelli. I thought maybe you could help me figure out what I should do. I've tried talking to Lisa, but she won't listen. She says she's going to get a divorce and I can't let that happen. I love her."

Josephine's tone softened. "My daughter is stubborn and headstrong, Alex. She always has been. And Lisa's never paid any attention to what I or my husband tell her, so I'm not sure what you think I can do."

"I need an ally. I need someone to talk to Lisa and try to convince her to stay in our marriage and work it out."

The dismay on the older woman's face didn't bode well for Alex. "I tried that once. I spoke to my daughter until I was blue in the face, trying to make her see that she was making a big mistake. But would she listen? These young women of today think they know everything."

Josephine shook her head. "I'll be honest with you. I wasn't happy that you and Lisa married outside the Catholic Church, but a marriage is sacred, no matter if

Elvis performs the ceremony or not. It would have been better with a priest, though."

"Just so you know, the Las Vegas thing wasn't my idea."

"You don't have to tell me that, Alex. Don't you think I know my daughter by now? This is a woman who dated a transvestite and didn't see a problem with it."

Alex's jaw dropped. "Really? I didn't know that."

"There's probably a lot about Lisa that you don't know. But she's a good girl with a good head on her shoulders. She just needs to use it. And I know she loves you."

His heart filled with hope. "Did she say that?"

"She didn't have to. A mother knows these things. And you forget that I'm a woman, too. Don't I know what a woman is thinking? Don't I know my own daughter?"

"What should I do?"

"You do what any man does when he wants a woman—you must sweep Lisa off her feet. And you'd better use a very big broom. That girl is as stubborn as they come."

6

"I'VE GOT A HOT DATE TONIGHT, so you might want to make yourself scarce." Leo preened and pirouetted around the kitchen in his new green silk shirt. "Don't I look wonderful? I just bought this. It's so me."

Grinning at her roommate, Lisa paused in the salad she was preparing for dinner, happy to have something other than Alex to occupy her mind.

She'd thought of little else since her husband's impromptu visit that morning, especially how yummy he'd looked, which wasn't at all fair to a woman who was finding celibacy a rather irksome state of affairs.

"So tell me everything. Are you going out with Peter again? Or is it someone new?" Leo's dance card was always full, making Lisa feel even more like a wallflower.

"His name is Bruce, and he's too adorable for words. I think I'm in love."

She rolled her eyes. "You think you're in love every week, Leo. I think you're confusing it with lust."

Shrugging, he picked out sliced cucumber from the greens and stuffed it into his mouth. "Bruce is an auto mechanic, very rugged and virile." He fanned himself dramatically and started singing *Macho Man*.

"He's not your type at all, Leo. I take it you met him when you took your car in to be serviced yesterday. Not exactly the kind of servicing you expected, huh?"

Leo grinned. "Oooh, naughty girl! I'm expanding my horizons, so to speak. I mean there's nothing wrong with dating a man in the trades, now is there? I just hope his fingernails are clean. I have a real problem with dirty nails." He shuddered, and Lisa almost laughed.

"I've never met an auto mechanic with clean nails, so your love affair may be short-lived. Of course, you can always insist that Bruce wear gloves. That should go over really well."

"Speaking of love affairs, Francie tells me that Alex put in an unexpected appearance this morning. I'm sure that was difficult for you to handle. Do you want to talk about it?"

Lisa sighed. "Not really. It's over between me and Alex, so what's the point?"

"The sadness in your voice tells me differently, sweetie. And if he's still in love with you, and you're still in love with him, then why don't you give your marriage another try? You owe it to yourselves and that grand institution."

"You are such a sentimental sap, Leo," Lisa said, patting her friend's cheek affectionately. In the short time they'd lived together, Lisa had grown very fond of her male roommate.

She'd had plenty of boyfriends during her lifetime— too many, in fact—but she'd never had a genuine platonic male relationship, until Leo. The fact that he was gay took all the pressure off their friendship. She could relax around him and talk to him as if he was just one of the girls. He was kind, had great insight and a terrific sense of humor. As soon as she broke him of his Mr. Clean complex, he'd be perfect.

"Just because Alex decided to visit doesn't mean anything. I asked myself, as I asked him, why he hadn't bothered to come around before."

"And what did he say?"

"That he was giving me time to get over my anger. It was such a crock, I nearly vomited."

"Makes sense to me."

"You men always stick together."

"Now, sweetie, I've been accused of many things, but never of being part of some mysterious men's club." He winked at her. "You know my loyalties are with you and your sister.

"Heaven forbid that anything should happen between Francie and Mark, but as much as I adore Mark, I would have to take Francie's side."

"Those two are solid as a rock. Nothing's going to happen to them. They have the perfect marriage." Lisa glanced up in alarm at Leo's heavy sigh. "What is it you're not telling me? Has Francie said something?"

The blond man hesitated momentarily, then shook his head. "No, nothing concrete. It's just that Francie seems sad lately. Have you noticed? She's not been focusing on work, as she should. I'm concerned that things aren't what they appear to be between Francie and Mark."

"Oh, Leo, you're just like an old woman. I think you worry more than my mother. Josephine has cornered the market on angst."

"I love Francie. I want her to be happy. And though I know she's deliriously in love with Mark, I still sense that there's something not quite right between those two," Leo insisted.

Lisa digested her friend's comments. "You have good instincts, Leo, so I'll talk to Francie tomorrow. Mark's going out of town on assignment *again*—" which could account for part of the problem, if there, in fact, was one "—and she's coming over for dinner. We'll have a chance to talk then."

"Thanks, sweetie. I knew I could count on you. And you won't tell Francie that I'm the one who put you up to it, will you? She'd be furious if she knew and I can't afford to have her quit."

"What will you do when she and Mark move to Bucks County? It's only a matter of time before they find a house they like and can afford, you know."

"I've given that a lot of thought." His expression grew animated. "I'm going to open up a second store and put Francie in charge of it, make her a full partner. You'll move into her position at the store here in town."

Lisa's eyes widened, and she felt a surge of nausea. "But, Leo! I've just started working at Designing

Women. I'm not an interior designer, and I haven't a clue about what it is you and Francie do."

"So you'll learn. We all have to start somewhere, right?"

Though Lisa nodded, she just wasn't sure.

No surprise there! She wasn't sure about anything these days, including what else to put in her salad.

"I'M GLAD WE HAVE THE ENTIRE evening all to ourselves, France. With Mark out of town and Leo on a date with Bruce, the ball-bearing king, it's just us girls."

The four weeks since she'd been back in Philadelphia had flown by, and Lisa hadn't had much opportunity to spend quality time with her sister. Even at work, both women were so busy they rarely had time to sit down and chat.

Francie continued pushing the peas around her plate in a distracted fashion. "That's nice."

Lisa had prepared meatloaf, mashed potatoes and peas—one of her sister's favorite dinners. She knew something was wrong, and she didn't think it was the food. "What's the matter? Don't you like my cooking anymore? I'll have you know I made this meal especially for you."

Francie looked up from her plate and her cheeks reddened. "I love your cooking, Lisa. You know that. You're a fabulous cook. And I don't mean to seem ungrateful, it's just that..." She heaved a dispirited sigh. "I'm not very hungry, I guess."

Lisa set down her fork. "Not hungry? Now that's a

crock if ever I heard one. You could eat the soles off shoes on a good day.

"Care to tell me what's bothering you? Are you and Mark having problems already?" Maybe Leo had been right. *Damn!*

Francie shook her head. "Not problems, exactly. It's just... Well, Mark wants to wait awhile before having a baby. He's pretty adamant about it, and—"

"And what? I thought that's what you both had decided, and it seems like a wise idea."

"I went off my birth control pills, and Mark doesn't know. He'll kill me when he finds out."

Lisa's eyes widened. "Holy shit! Are you sure that's such a smart thing to do, France? I mean, having a kid should be a mutual decision, right?"

"I know, but Mark kept talking about waiting a year or two. And I don't want to wait that long. I'm not getting any younger, you know."

"What are you, closing in on thirty? For chrissake, Francie! You're hardly a dried-up old prune. Did Mom put you up to going off your pills? I smell her hand in this."

"No, for once this is all my idea. Mom had nothing to do with it, except for her usual questioning about when was I going to give her a grandchild."

"Are you pregnant? Is that the reason you've been distracted and moody lately?"

Shaking her head, Francie's eyes filled with tears. "That's just the problem. I got my period yesterday. I was so hoping that..."

The admission filled Lisa with relief. She didn't want Francie and Mark's marriage to end up like hers. And dishonesty was the first step to divorce. "You dodged a bullet, if you ask me. Mark would be pissed if he discovered your duplicity, and rightly so."

Thank goodness Lisa had been spared the problem of pregnancy. At least, she hoped she'd been spared. She still hadn't gotten her period, which was due, most likely, to all the stress she'd been under lately.

That's what she kept telling herself, anyway.

"I know. I'm just so miserable. I mean, I love Mark more than anything, but my biological clock has gone haywire. It's totally out of whack. Every time I see a woman pushing a baby stroller, I come unglued."

"You need to talk to Mark about this, France. Explain how you feel, how important having a baby is to you. He's a reasonable guy—"

"Isn't that an oxymoron?"

"In most cases, yes, but not when it comes to Mark. The man choked on humble pie to get you to marry him. I don't think he's going to mess things up now. He loves you too much."

Reaching her hand out, Francie clasped her sister's. "When did you get so wise? I'm supposed to be the older, smarter sister, you know."

"Wise? *Ha!* That's rich. I couldn't keep my own marriage together and you think I'm wise? I've lost the only man I'll ever love. How wise is that?"

There! She'd admitted it. She loved Alex. So what? Nothing was going to change between them.

"Alex isn't lost, Lisa. He loves you. You're the one who tossed him aside, not the other way around. It's not too late to get him back."

"Correction. He tossed me—to the wolves. Only the wolves were rich, wore Armani, and were called Mackenzie."

"You need to forgive your husband. You'll be miserable for the rest of your life, if you don't."

"Too late! I'm already miserable, so what's the point of compounding the problem? Alex and I just weren't meant to be."

"Now who's spewing trash? That's the stupidest thing I've heard you say since you've returned home. Maybe Alex is guilty of being dense. He is a man, after all. And maybe you used poor judgment when you decided to sneak away like a thief in the night. I don't know. But what I do know is that he loves you and you love him, so quit being so stubborn and irrational."

"You weren't there, Francie. And I'm supposed to be giving the advice tonight, not you."

Shaking her head, Francie smiled softly. "Do you think we Morelli girls suffer from some kind of curse? We certainly have our share of problems when it comes to men."

Lisa grimaced. "Hello? Hell, yes, we're cursed! Look who we have as a role model."

"What do you mean?" her sister asked, eyebrows drawing together. "Mom and Dad have a good marriage. They've been together forever and are very happy."

"What I mean is that Mom is a strong, self-reliant woman who exerts her independence whenever she feels the need, which, unfortunately, is often. And she's passed those traits on to us, admirable or not. We didn't·stand a chance. Our genes were tainted from the get-go."

Francie heaved a sigh. "So we are cursed."

"It certainly seems so, doesn't it?"

THE FOLLOWING NIGHT, Lisa, clad in her faded blue-flannel pajamas, was just snuggling down in front of the tube with a quart of her favorite Ben & Jerry's when the doorbell rang.

She knew it wasn't Leo, who was out with Bruce again, despite the man's atrocious vocabulary, or lack thereof, and his desperate need for a wardrobe make-over.

Fastidious Leo had plans to redo Bruce into a won-drous specimen of mankind, though Lisa wasn't sure it was possible. It was that whole sow's ear–silk purse thing, and she thought there was just too much sow and not enough silk to deal with.

"Open the door, Lisa! It's your mother."

"Oh, shit!" Groaning audibly, Lisa made a face, re-lieved it wasn't Alex, but just as horrified that her mother was paying a call.

Josephine Morelli's visits never brought good news. She was like the grim reaper—sadness and despair fol-lowed wherever she traveled. This Terminator's atti-tude was far worse than Arnold's!

"Hi, Mom!" Lisa said upon opening the door, doing her best to look cheerful though her smile felt pasted on, or maybe that was dried ice cream.

"It's kinda late for a visit, isn't it?" She glanced at her wristwatch. "It's nearly eight o'clock. Aren't you missing reruns of *The Golden Girls*?"

"They're not on tonight, and your father's playing poker with his friends, so I decided to get some fresh air."

Lisa's eyes widened. "You walked? That's kinda far, isn't it?" Her parents lived in the Little Italy section of Philadelphia.

"No, I drove. But I left the window open a crack. It isn't safe for a woman to be walking the streets alone at night. Rapists, you know. Even a woman my age has to be careful. Rape is not about sex. It's about violence against—"

"Ma, I've read the literature, okay? So, what brings you to Rittenhouse Square?"

"I'm visiting my daughter, is that a crime? Maybe you could offer me some of that ice cream I see smeared all over your pajama top. I didn't have my dessert tonight and I'm hungry for something sweet."

Josephine's sweet tooth put Leo's to shame.

"Sure. Have a seat in the living room. I'll get you a bowl, and—"

Josephine shook her head. "I'd rather sit in the kitchen, if you don't mind. Leo's fancy furniture makes me nervous. I'm afraid I might spill something."

Lisa dismissed her mother's objection with a flick of

her wrist. "I got over that the first day I lived here by turning over the seat cushion. I figure I'll have it cleaned before I move."

"You'd better be careful. The man might kick you out and then where will you live?"

"Why, with you, of course. Wouldn't that be fun?" *Not!!*

"You know you're always welcome."

Lisa placed a bowl of ice cream in front of her mother, helped herself to seconds, then sat at the table across from her. "Okay, what is it? I know this isn't a social call. You don't make social calls, Mom."

Ulterior motives were Josephine's specialty, as were guilt trips. A person could ride for days on one of her mother's guilt trips and never reach their intended destination. Of course, by the end of the journey they'd be suicidal!

"*Mmm.* This is very good ice cream. What's it called?"

"Cherry Garcia. Now what is it you want to talk to me about? And don't tell me ice cream, because I'm not buying it."

"Alex came to see me."

"Oh, for chrissake! Why am I not surprised? I knew it had to be something like that."

"You should watch your language, young lady. Alex was very upset that you're thinking of divorcing him. What else was the poor man to do? The boy needs help. He's like a lost soul, so he came to see me."

Lisa fought the urge to gag. Not for a minute did she

believe that Alex was as pathetic as her mother painted him to be. The man had obviously done a number on her, just as he'd done on Lisa.

"Mom, no offense, but I don't think there's anything you or anyone else can do. We've had this talk already, remember? I thought you had accepted my decision to end my marriage."

"I never accepted it, Lisa. I tried to talk sense into you then and it's my duty to try and talk sense to you now. Alex loves you. He doesn't want to lose you. You have a duty, both to him and to the church, to try and make a go of this marriage."

"First of all, I didn't get married in the Catholic Church, and I doubt that clown-of-a-preacher who performed the ceremony gives a rat's ass. I don't owe Alex a damn thing."

"But, Lisa, he—"

Lisa heaved a sigh. "It's too late, Mom. Alex should have thought of the consequences when his parents were insulting the hell out of me and he said nothing in my defense. I expected more of him. I should have had more, as his wife, but instead I got bubkes."

"Alex feels terrible about it. He told me so."

Lisa's eyebrow shot up. "Well, that's something, I guess. But that doesn't change anything. We're too different. We just don't have enough in common. I knew that when I married him, but I ignored it. Love, as they say, is blind."

"So you admit that you love him." Josephine's face lit up and she clapped her hands together. "I knew it!"

"Yes, I still love Alex, but it changes nothing. I'm moving on with my life, and so should Alex. He'll go back to Florida and work with his father, and—"

Josephine shook her head, a triumphant look on her face, as if she were holding the trump card in a high-stakes card game. "Alex is not going back to Florida, Lisa. Apparently, his decision to come back for you caused a rift with his family. He's resigned from his father's company and is going to open up his own mortgage business here in Philadelphia."

The air left Lisa's lungs. "What?" That was an eventuality she hadn't counted on.

Alex had spent most of his life trying to live up to his father's expectations. It was the one thing they had in common, though, for the most part, he had succeeded while Lisa had failed.

Josephine nodded. "That's what he told me. We had a very frank discussion and he confided in me. I am his mother-in-law, after all. Some people respect an older person's opinion."

"Alex didn't mention any of this when he came to see me the other day."

"Would you have listened?"

Lisa thought over the question carefully. "Probably not. Anyway, it really doesn't make a difference to me. My mind's made up."

Josephine heaved a dispirited sigh. "I raised you to be an intelligent and independent woman, Lisa. I can see that you're only using half of what you learned.

You should start listening more to your heart. That's where the truth lies."

"As you pointed out, Ma, I'm a grown woman, and I have to do what I think is best."

Her mother's response was to let loose a few colorful Italian expletives. "You're making a big mistake. I can feel it in my heart that you'll live to regret this decision."

"The only mistake I made was falling in love with Alex and marrying him in the first place. But I plan to rectify that, and soon."

"And if there's a child?"

"There won't be."

"Are you telling me that you got your period?"

"Well, no. But I'm sure I'm not pregnant. I have no symptoms."

"But what if you are?"

"I'm not, okay? So let's drop it."

But Josephine didn't look convinced.

And neither was Lisa.

7

It was Saturday night and Lisa had decided that she'd done enough staying at home. Tonight was her debut back into the world of dating.

She was single—*well, sort of single*—and attractive. And she wasn't going to stay at home and brood about Alexander Mackenzie. She'd done enough of that already. Now, she was going to have fun.

Not to mention that the batteries in her vibrator had died ages ago.

There were a lot of available men in Philadelphia, and Lisa intended to find herself one or two. Hell, in the mood she was in, she might decide to take on the entire Philadelphia Eagles football team.

Dressed to thrill in a short black sleeveless dress that showed off her body to perfection, fishnet stockings and stiletto heels guaranteed to horrify any podiatrist worth his salt, Lisa took one last look in the mirror, winked at her reflection and sucked in her breath.

Club Zero had always been lucky for her—well, except for the night she had met Alex—and she planned to meet her best friend Molly Malloy there and check out the action.

"Nothing ventured, nothing gained," she told herself before heading out of the apartment.

Molly was seated at their usual table and waved at Lisa as soon as she entered the noisy nightclub. Not that Lisa needed a flag to find her friend; she needed only to look for the vibrant red hair, outlandish clothes and big engaging smile.

Lisa had known Molly since junior high school and they had always been the best of friends, sharing all the important firsts—first bra, first period, and the ever popular loss of virginity. Molly had actually gone first on that one.

"Hey, Molls," Lisa said, sliding into the seat next to her. "You're looking pretty outrageous this evening. Like the outfit."

Molly was dressed in fifties mode tonight, from the crown of her lavender pillbox, complete with face netting, to the pristine purple-and-pink flowered shirtwaist dress, cinched with a matching belt. On her feet she wore pink anklets and patent-leather heels, and beneath it all a stiffly starched net petticoat.

The woman was either going to attract someone crazy in love with Donna Reed or a child molester.

"Do you like it?" Molly asked, grinning. "I wasn't sure if it was too over-the-top for fifties night, but then I figured, what the hell, why not?"

"I feel dowdy by comparison," Lisa replied, reaching for the Fuzzy Navel the waitress had just delivered and taking a sip. Lisa matched her drinks to her mood, and since she was hot-wired tonight, a Navel was just the ticket to get things going.

"How's the action?"

"Same as always," Molly raised her voice in an effort to be heard above the din as Bill Haley's "Rock Around the Clock" blared from the jukebox. "I've seen a few new faces, and I thought I recognized one that was familiar. Don't turn around too quickly, but isn't that your soon-to-be ex-husband sitting at the end of the bar?"

"Shit, I hope not!" Sucking in her breath, Lisa turned her head slowly. "I was looking forward to having some fun tonight." But that didn't seem possible now. The sight of Alex, head lowered over his drink, looking as forlorn as an abandoned puppy, made her heart twitch.

Damn! Why did he have to show up tonight?

"He's been sitting there since before you came in. By the looks of him, he's not feeling any pain."

"Alex's specialty is inflicting pain, not feeling any himself." That wasn't quite true. She'd seen pain reflected in his eyes on those occasions when his father was overly critical of his work performance.

"Just thought I'd warn you, in case you want to change your mind and go somewhere else," Molly said. "I understand if you do."

Despite her disclaimer, Lisa could see that Molly would be disappointed. "Why should I leave? Alex and I have been separated for five weeks, and I've told him how it's going to be from here on out. And besides, this is a free country. I'm not going to be chased away from my favorite hangout because he's decided to come here, too."

Her friend smiled in relief. "That's good. Because Alan Parker is heading in your direction and it looks like he's going to ask you to dance."

"I thought Alan was still in jail for driving with a suspended license."

"Yeah, well, you know Alan. That man could talk his way out of a death sentence, he's that good of a salesman."

Alan Parker embodied the three Ps: persistent, pretentious and problematic. He wasn't Lisa's type, at all. But since she wasn't looking for anything even remotely smacking of a relationship, and Alan did have a decent sense of humor, he fit the bill for a fun, no-strings-attached evening.

And Lisa had heard from a few of her friends that he was pretty good in bed—not that she was interested. Even though she was horny, Alan just didn't do it for her. Plus, she suspected that Molly had a crush on him.

"Hey, Lisa! You're looking good tonight. You, too, Molly. I like the getup. But isn't it a little early for Halloween?"

"Nice seeing you, too, Alan. I'm outta here," the annoyed woman said to Lisa, shaking her head. "I'll be at the bar. Let me know when you get rid of the Fonz."

Molly's jibe didn't fool Lisa, and it didn't faze Alan in the least. "Shall we dance? It's fifties night and I'm eager to rock and roll." Danny and the Juniors "At The Hop" started playing.

"I'm not very good at the bop, Alan. I think I'll pass." It was a lie. Lisa was an excellent dancer, but she wasn't in the mood tonight. Alex's unexpected appearance had ruined that.

"Oh, come on. It'll be fun. I promise not to show you up too badly."

Like that was even a remote possibility, Lisa thought, knowing she could not refuse the challenge.

WATCHING LISA OUT ON the dance floor, twisting and shouting with some guy dressed up to look like Elvis, Alex's heart sank somewhere to the vicinity of his knees as memories of their unorthodox wedding day flooded over him.

Her dance partner was wearing a black-leather jacket and tight blue jeans. His dark hair was slicked back and long sideburns flanked his cheeks.

Alex wondered if this was the kind of man Lisa was attracted to, because she sure as hell didn't seem attracted to him anymore.

Of course, Alex wasn't the blue-jeans type. Never had been. He was conservative in his dress and manner, which apparently didn't suit the women of today, who wanted wild not Wall Street.

Lisa looked incredibly hot in the short black dress she wore. Her legs were long and shapely, and damn sexy in those mile-high heels. It was obvious that she wasn't wearing a bra, and that fact didn't sit well with Alex, not at all.

Taking a sip of Glenmorangie, his eyes widened as yet another man dragged his wife across the dance floor. This one had on skintight black pants, no shirt and a clerical collar fastened around his neck. Someone had called him "The Preacher," but he didn't look like any clergyman Alex had ever seen.

Apparently Lisa liked him; she was laughing, singing and planting kisses on his cheeks, and the sight filled Alex with jealous anger.

Jealousy had been an alien emotion before now—before he had fallen in love with Lisa.

Like should seek like, his mother had always professed. And there was some truth to that, because the differences between someone as carefree and wild as Lisa and as conservative and levelheaded as Alex drove him to the brink of insanity.

Eyes narrowed, he cursed loudly before downing his scotch. Slipping off the bar stool, Alex decided that he'd had just about enough of his wife's antics and intended to confront the aggravating woman.

"Lisa!" he shouted, weaving his way through the crowded dance floor on unsteady feet. Reaching her, he clasped her arm, which she tried to pull back.

"Come on. We're leaving. I've seen enough. It's time we went home and got this straightened out."

Her eyes widened, but not in fear. If anything, she looked pissed beyond belief. "I'm not going anywhere with you, Alex. Now let go of my arm."

The Preacher stepped between them and pushed Alex back. "The lady said no. Now why don't you take the hint and get lost, or I'm going to have to perform last rites."

"She's my wife!"

"According to Lisa that's a mere technicality. Now beat it. We're dancing here."

Before he knew what was happening, two massively built bouncers grabbed Alex by the arms, lifted him off the ground and escorted him out the door, depositing him none-too-gently onto the sidewalk.

"Go sober up before you get yourself into real trouble, buddy," one of them said before shutting the door behind him.

Having never before been ejected from an establishment of any type, Alex felt totally humiliated, not to mention completely asinine as his butt warmed the cold pavement.

If this is what loving someone does to you, then maybe I should just rethink the whole damn thing!

LISA HURRIED OUT THE DOOR of the nightclub into the chilly night air to find her husband sprawled on the sidewalk.

Worried that he might be hurt, she bent over to help him to his feet. "What are you doing here, Alex? I hope you haven't been following me again."

"I'm sweeping you off your feet. Didn't you notice?" He brushed the dirt off his pants. "Apparently, I'm not doing a very good job of it."

"Your first mistake was listening to my mother, the second was not listening to me. Now go home and sleep it off. You've obviously had too much to drink. Things will be clearer in the morning."

"I haven't had too much to drink. Two scotches, that's it."

She arched an eyebrow in disbelief. "Did you have dinner beforehand?"

Alex shook his head. "No. Come to think of it, I didn't. I haven't had much of an appetite lately."

"Well, no wonder then. Where's your car? You're in no shape to drive."

He pointed to a blue Dodge Intrepid. "It's a rental."

Lisa held out her hand. "Give me the keys. I'll drive you to your friend's apartment."

"You don't have to do that, Lisa. I can manage. I'm perfectly fine." He swayed a bit, and she reached out to steady him. When she did, Alex grabbed Lisa and drew her to his chest, planting his lips firmly over hers in a mind-melting kiss that seemed to go on forever.

Lisa forgot to breathe. She'd forgotten how wonderfully narcotic Alex's kisses were. She'd forgotten how the mere feel of his lips next to hers made her knees grow weak and her mind go numb.

She'd forgotten what a bastard he was.

Pulling back, she ordered, "Stop it, Alex! Stop trying to woo me back. It's not going to work."

"I'm not sorry for kissing you. And I'm not drunk, if that's what you think."

"Get real. And get in. Because you're not driving

home in your condition. I'll not have your death on my conscience."

"That's nice of you," he said with no small amount of sarcasm.

"Don't mention it. It's the least I can do since my mother probably put you up to this foolishness."

"She didn't. Well, not exactly."

Pulling away from the curb, Lisa asked, "How did you know I'd be at the club tonight? I don't remember telling anyone, except Molly, my plans."

"I've been at the club every night this week, waiting for you to show. I figured I'd get lucky at some point."

She found his admission oddly touching, not to mention, disconcerting. "So you weren't following me?"

Alex shook his head and a lopsided grin escaped. "Not this time, love."

"I'm not your love. Don't call me that."

"Now, Lisa, be reasonable. I love you, you're my love, and I know deep down that you love me, too. You just aren't willing to admit it right now."

Damn you, Josephine Morelli!

"You shouldn't listen to anything my mother has to say. She's demented, a serial busybody." She gripped the steering wheel harder. "By the way, where am I taking you?"

Alex issued directions to Bill Connor's apartment, and then said, "Bill's out of town. Would you like to come up for a cup of coffee? I promise to behave."

After that kiss—that wonderfully, wild, erotic kiss he had given her, Lisa was tempted, but knew full well where it would lead. When it came to Alex, her will-power just wasn't what it should be.

"That's not a good idea." She pulled the car to a halt in front of the brick apartment complex he indicated. "Besides, Molly and Alan are waiting for me. It would be rude not to return." Though Molly, who she knew would relish the chance to be alone with Alan, would be grateful for her absence.

"Please stay! I want to talk to you."

There was no way Lisa was going to put herself into such a compromising situation. A cup of coffee would lead to another kiss, then an embrace and finally, to bed.

The sex would be fabulous, but Lisa wasn't playing that game. Not anymore.

"I'm sorry, but I don't think we have anything left to talk about. Go upstairs to bed, Alex. I'll park your car outside the club. You can take a cab and pick it up to-morrow. I'll leave the keys with the bartender and ex-plain the situation."

"Fine. But I'm not giving up, Lisa. I love you. How long is it going to take for me to convince you of that?"

"Longer than you have, I'm afraid. Goodbye, Alex."

"Not goodbye," he insisted. "Just good night. In the immortal words of Arnold, 'I'll be back.'"

Swallowing her smile at his stupid impersonation, Lisa was surprised that Alex had ever seen a Termina-tor movie.

"I think this is the scene where you dissolve, Alex. See ya."

JOSEPHINE HAD HAD QUITE enough of her daughter's stubborn refusal to patch things up with her husband.

No good would come of Lisa's decision to divorce Alex, she was positive of that. And Josephine prided herself on rarely being wrong.

Didn't her daughter realize that marriage was hard work and, more importantly, that a baby might have resulted from her union with Alexander Mackenzie?

Josephine's heart fluttered at the very idea of becoming a grandmother. It was something she had longed for over the years. But her daughters had not been eager to marry and settle down, and she had no bambinos to show for their stubbornness.

What was wrong with these young women of today?

"Disposable society," her husband, John, always said, and he was right. Everything was just too easy to toss away, including marriage.

"I'm going to call Lisa's mother-in-law and ask her to help me get Alex and Lisa back together," Josephine told her mother, who was seated at the kitchen table, busy shoving sausage and peppers into her mouth.

Loretta Abrizzi was somewhere between the ages of eighty and ninety years old. No one was really positive of her actual birth date, including her two daughters, Josephine and Florence. She was still a feisty old girl, though she was losing a bit of her mental facilities as the weeks and months went by.

Looking up from her lunch, the old woman paused and crossed herself. "This is not a good idea, Josephine," she said. "Your daughter will not appreciate your interference. Lisa is all grown-up now and knows her own mind."

"That's rich coming from you, Ma. All you've done your entire life is interfere in mine. And now I'm not supposed to get involved when my daughter is in trouble?"

"Times have changed. Women are different now."

"I don't care. I'm not going to sit by and allow Lisa to ruin her life. She loves Alex, and he loves her. And he asked for my help. It's my duty to do something."

Lisa's grandmother swallowed her wine, wiped her lips with a napkin, and then said, "You cannot live their lives for them, Josie. As much as you want to help, you will cause trouble in the family if you do. You may even lose your daughter. You know how much she hates those people. You said yourself Alex's parents reminded you of Mussolini." Not a fan of the dictator, Grandma pretended to spit on the floor.

"Maybe so. But Miriam Mackenzie is responsible for breaking my Lisa's heart, not to mention breaking up her marriage. And by all that is holy, she will be the one to help put it back together, or I will have you put the evil eye on her."

The evil eye was used only in rare circumstances, and then only against Josephine's most hated enemy. Evoking the curse had been known to render virile men impotent, fertile women barren, and occasionally could cause warts to appear for no reason.

"I haven't used the evil eye in years," Grandma Abrizzi admitted. "I'm not sure I can still do it."

Clutching her chest, she moaned. "Quick! Get the antacid. You're giving me heartburn."

Reaching into one of the cupboards, Josephine placed the Mylanta in front of her mother. "That's from the sausage and peppers. I told you if you ate them you'd be sorry. But would you listen? You're as stubborn as your granddaughter. And you can't lose the ability to give the evil eye—it's an inherited gift."

"Then why don't you do it?"

"Because I wasn't born with the ability, though there have been times when I wished—" She shook her head.

"Sometimes I wonder why that husband of yours puts up with you. You're a bossy woman who talks too much."

"Which means I'm just like you, Ma, so don't be insulting me. You're only insulting yourself."

"*Bah!* One day your daughters will turn on you, as you have turned on me, and you'll know what it's like to grow old."

"I already know. You and the girls are driving me to an early grave. First, Francie with those four weddings, which cost me a pretty penny, I can tell you, and now Lisa, who runs off and marries a man she hardly knows, in Las Vegas of all places. How can a marriage be blessed in a sinful place like that?"

"I liked Elvis. Sure, he had a few problems, and a big fat belly, but he was a good guy, gave lotsa money to charity. And I hear he was a fan of Sinatra. So Frank was connected to the Mob, nobody's perfect."

"Where's the gratitude I deserve?" Josephine went on, ignoring her mother. Most old Italian ladies liked Mario Lanza or, God forbid, Eddie Fisher, but not Loretta Abrizzi. She was an Elvis and Sinatra fan from way back.

"I should be doting on my grandchildren right now, not worrying about my daughters and their marriages." Francie seemed distracted of late, and her behavior also worried Josephine.

"It's a mother's job to worry. You don't think I worry about you getting too fat and dropping dead before I do? A mother shouldn't outlive her children. It's not the way God intended."

Josephine's eyes narrowed into thin slits. "You think I'm fat? I only ate half of what you did for lunch."

"I'm an old woman. I have no husband to keep interested. I'm just saying you should watch it."

"John loves me just the way I am. He's told me so many times."

"What a man says and what a man does are two different things. And if that's so, why is he always going off to be with his *goombahs?* Or maybe he's got a chippie on the side, and you don't know about her. A man his age gets the wandering eye. Your father had it." Loretta crossed herself, in memory of her dead husband.

Josephine's mouth fell open. "Are you nuts? Papa never cheated on you. He was the salt of the earth."

"No, but he thought about it. Once in his sleep he called out the name Lucia. Our next-door neighbor was

Lucia Mozarelli. She was a *puttana*, but her breasts were large and the men liked her.''

It finally dawned on Josephine that the conversation she was having with her mother made absolutely no sense. "Why are you telling me all this? What's it got to do with Lisa's problem? Alex is not cheating on her, I'm certain of that.''

Loretta thought for a moment, her forehead wrinkling in confusion. "Who's Lisa? I don't know any Alex.''

Letting loose a string of curses, Josephine shook her hand at the Almighty and went in search of Miriam Mackenzie's phone number.

One crackpot was all she could handle in a day, and now she'd be saddled with two.

8

"WHAT'S WRONG, LISA? You've been down in the mouth this entire week. Is it because of that run-in you had with your husband at the nightclub last Saturday night?"

Lisa shrugged, handing her sister the swatches of material she'd requested for a new customer who was due in later that morning. "It's true. I can't stop thinking about Alex. But I don't think it's just that." She heaved a sigh.

Francie's face filled with concern. "Then what is it? You can tell me."

"I don't mean to sound ungrateful, Francie, but I don't think I'm really happy doing this job. I don't find it challenging, and I'm not sure working at Designing Women is what I want to spend the rest of my life doing." She shut her eyes, afraid to see the disappointment in her sister's.

But Francie was more surprised than angry. "But you're doing such a wonderful job. Leo told me just the other day that he was impressed with your initiative and was going to give you a raise. And it's not easy to impress Leo, I'll have you know. He's very picky. If it's the money, I can—"

"It's not about money. I just feel there's something missing from my life, that I'm supposed to be doing something other than pulling swatches and making deliveries. I know I've made some poor choices over the years, like the exotic-dancing thing, but this job isn't working, either. Maybe it's just me. I don't seem to fit in anywhere."

Her father had told Lisa once that she was a square peg in a round world. Now she knew what he meant.

"You know delivering and fetching materials won't last forever. Leo plans to move you up to a designer position, once you learn the ropes."

"But that's just it. I don't think I want to learn the ropes." Lisa shook her head. "Oh, hell. I don't know what I want. My failed marriage is a perfect example of that. I just can't do anything right."

"Stop talking like that. You're being entirely too negative about yourself." Francie clasped her sister's hand. "Tell you what. Why don't you walk down the street to Smollensky's and get me one of their fabulous crumb cakes. I didn't have breakfast this morning, and I've been craving one."

At the word *craving* Lisa gasped. "You're not pregnant, are you? Please tell me you're not. I know how much you want a baby, but Mark is going to freak out if he finds out you went and got pregnant behind his back."

Shaking her head, Francie smiled. "I'm not pregnant. Not yet, anyway. But I took your advice and had a heart to heart talk with Mark, just the other night. I told him exactly how I feel. He's had a change of heart and wants me to get pregnant, says he thought it over and all his previous objections seem stupid to him now."

Smart man, Lisa thought, hugging her sister. "That's great, Francie! I'm so happy for you. What happens now?"

"Why just the usual morning, noon and night stuff, until we conceive."

"I bet Mark's a happy man these days."

"He just grins and bears it. A man's gotta do what a man's gotta do, is his new motto. And he does it so well."

Pulling a five-dollar bill from her wallet, Francie handed it to Lisa. "Here, this is for the cake. Don't come back without it, or I may go into a frenzy. When you return, we'll talk about your options for the future. How does that sound?"

"All right. Two heads are better than one, I guess. And I can do with a Smollensky fix myself right about now."

SMOLLENSKY'S BAKERY was as much a fixture in Philadelphia as the Liberty Bell.

Lisa and her family had been shopping there for years. Bread, rolls, bear claws or birthday cakes, if you wanted the best, you bought your bakery goods from Sol Smollensky.

Sol was older than God—or so it had always seemed to Lisa—with a thin patch of white hair on the top of his head, a large round belly protruding from beneath his not-so-pristine white apron and a smile that could light up an entire room. He'd lost his wife a year previously to cancer and didn't smile as much these days. His teeth were false and clacked when he spoke, but that was the only thing fake about the kindhearted baker. If Sol told you something, you could bank on it.

Inhaling deeply, Lisa moved toward the counter, smiling at the older man. "How's it going today, Sol?"

"Can't complain. Business has been okay. Not great, but okay."

Her forehead furrowed. "Why not great? You've got the best bakery goods in town." She gazed longingly at the prettily decorated Valentine's cookies. "This place should be packed." She turned her head, noticing for the first time that she was Sol's only customer, which was strange. The bakery should have been crowded at this time of day.

Sol shrugged. "We got competition from all the big grocery-store chains now, not to mention the discount clubs. They've all got bakeries, and they can sell cheaper than I can. It was only a matter of time until we started to feel the pinch."

"Their stuff isn't as good as yours. Maybe you need to advertise more."

"Maybe I need to retire. I'm getting too old to be working so hard. I don't enjoy it as much as I used to. And I'm starting to lose money. Man cannot live by bread alone, as they say. If I could, I'd be set for life, no?"

Lisa sighed, knowing exactly how the older man felt.

"So what brings you in today, Lisa? I got some nice éclairs, or maybe you'd like some blueberry muffins. I just took them out of the oven a few minutes ago." The tantalizing aroma of freshly baked muffins scented with vanilla and cinnamon filled the air.

"Francie wants a crumb cake, and I'll take as many blueberry muffins as you can give me for whatever's left of this five-dollar bill."

Sol pulled the familiar pink cardboard box with the Smollensky's gold-foil label from beneath the counter and began packing it with the streusel crumb cake. Lisa's stomach growled. Next he filled another box with six blueberry muffins and tied that up, as well. Lisa's stomach growled even louder.

"Smells scrumptious. I can't wait."

"I'm glad somebody appreciates my efforts. Since Olivia died, my heart hasn't been in the bakery business. I really am thinking about retiring."

Lisa gasped. "But you can't do that, Sol! You're an institution around here. Where would I buy my cookies and doughnuts? My sister is trying to get pregnant. She can't get pregnant if she doesn't have your crumb cake. You're important to a great many people, me included."

"So you'll come here a couple of days a week and I'll teach you how to bake what I bake, then you can make all the same cakes and pastries for your family and friends."

Eyes wide with incredulity, Lisa asked, "You would

do that for me, teach me your baking secrets?" This had to be a dream. But if it was, she didn't want to wake up. Learning how to bake professionally had been her innermost desire for years.

"Your mother's told me many times that she thought you were a very talented baker, Lisa, and Josephine always tells it like it is. One time she was too harsh about my bread being stale, but I've forgiven her."

"My mother said I was a talented baker? I had no idea she knew I loved to bake."

"Mothers know everything. As a woman, you should know that and be comforted by it."

Skeptical as to the veracity of the baker's statement, Lisa's eyebrows went up. "Maybe."

"So, do you want to learn how the professionals do it? It won't be easy. I can promise you that. Getting up at three in the morning is a killer. But I could use the help, if you think you can do it. I've got a touch of arthritis in my hands now and it makes kneading the dough difficult."

Lisa's face lit, and without a moment's hesitation, she nodded enthusiastically. The opportunity of a lifetime was being dropped in her lap, and she intended to make the most of it. "I can work weekends. I'm off on Saturdays and Sundays. Would that work?"

He nodded. "I'm open Saturday and a few hours on Sunday morning, for the church crowd. I quit the whole religious-thing myself, after Olivia died. I just didn't see the point. For God to have taken my wife..."

Sol shook his head. "It seemed like a great injustice had been done. She never harmed a soul."

The pain in the baker's eyes gave Lisa pause. How wonderful it would be, she thought, to be loved so completely and forever.

"Sometimes God wants the good ones with him, Sol. Maybe he needed Olivia's help up in Heaven. You know how she was always donating her time to one charity or another."

He seemed somewhat comforted by her words. "You're a good girl, Lisa. You come on Saturday and we'll bake. I think you've got what it takes to become a professional."

A WEEK LATER, Miriam Mackenzie faced her son's mother-in-law across a table at Starbucks. It was late in the morning and the restaurant was relatively empty of customers, save for the two women.

Josephine had picked the location on purpose, knowing that no one in her family frequented this establishment at this particular location. What she had to say to Miriam Mackenzie she wanted to say in private.

"Your husband didn't come with you?" Josephine asked, stirring sugar into her cup while she sized up her opponent. For all her furs, jewelry and fake smiles, Miriam Mackenzie appeared to be a steel magnolia, like the women in the movie that Josephine had watched so many times—soft on the outside but hard as steel within.

Alex's mother shook her head. "Rupert stayed at

home. I told him I was visiting an old friend from school. I thought it best to come alone. Your phone call sounded dire and mysterious. My husband has no patience for such drama and, I must admit, neither do I. So, I hope I haven't wasted my time by coming." Pinky out, she lifted her paper cup to her lips and sipped the hot coffee, as if she were entertaining the queen in her front parlor.

Josephine could practically smell the money seeping from this woman's pores. Mingled with the perfume she was wearing—Chanel, unless she missed her guess—it made her nauseous. "Since when is your son's happiness a waste of time? Most mothers wouldn't feel that way. I know I don't."

Miriam sighed. "If I thought Alexander had been truly happy married to your daughter, Mrs. Morelli, I might agree. But I think everything has turned out for the best. In time, you'll see that I'm right."

"I doubt that very much."

"Alex and Lisa are from two different worlds. Your daughter left, so she must have realized that, too. Lisa might not have had much polish, but she seemed to be a sensible young woman."

Gritting her teeth, Josephine counted to ten under her breath, and then replied, "My daughter left because she grew tired of you and your husband trying to sabotage her marriage. Lisa might be different, and she might not be as polished as the women you associate with, but she isn't a fool or a phony. She says what she believes and takes people at their word. She's not one to play games. In that, my daughter is a lot like me."

"That's all very interesting, but I came here because you indicated on the phone that it was a life-or-death situation. If my son is ill, or something bad has happened to him, I want to know and I want to know now."

"Alex was fine the last time I saw him, so you needn't worry about that."

"Well, thank God! And since you prefer the truth, I will tell you that I am greatly relieved that Alex and Lisa are contemplating divorce. Your daughter could never have made my son happy. Lisa, I fear, was a bit too unconventional for Alex."

Josephine cursed, and not beneath her breath this time. "Alex came to see me, to ask for my help. He loves Lisa and wants her back, unconventional or not. But she isn't willing to open herself up to the kind of abuse you and your husband heaped upon her and that your son tolerated."

Miriam's eyes reflected false innocence, and Josephine added, "Don't look so surprised. Did you think my daughter was so stupid that she didn't know what you were up to?"

"Why, I never—"

"Cut the act, Miriam. I believe Lisa. And the only reason I called you is that there is something bigger at stake here than you or I, or even Lisa and Alex."

The other woman's eyebrows drew together in confusion. "I don't understand what you're talking about."

"Do you know what happens when two people have sex?"

Miriam gasped, clutching her chest. "Why, I never— Mrs. Morelli, how dare you speak of such indelicate matters? I am a gently reared—"

"Stuff the Southern belle routine, okay? My daughter could very well be pregnant with your first grandchild. Have you given any thought to that? It's been seven weeks since Lisa left Florida. There could be a baby growing inside of her." Josephine could see by the stupefied expression on the woman's face that she hadn't.

"My first grandchild? But—"

"Please, don't ask me how that's possible. You gave birth to a son, so you should know already about the birds and bees." Miriam blushed as pink as the raspberry wool suit she wore.

"Lisa is almost two months late with her period. And though it's true that it could be from the stress of her breakup with Alex, I don't think it is. I'm positive she's going to have a baby. I feel it here." She patted her chest. "And if she is pregnant, then we must do everything in our power to get your son and my daughter back together. A child deserves two parents."

Alex's mother began fanning herself with a napkin, and Josephine shoved a glass of water at her. "But we don't know that for certain," Miriam said, looking withered and somewhat pale.

"Do you want to take that chance? If Lisa divorces Alex, and then has a baby, you will not be a part of that child's life. I know my daughter well enough to believe that. Not that I want my grandchild exposed to people like you and your husband, but I must do what's best for my daughter and help save this marriage. I wouldn't be a good mother if I didn't try."

"But what can I do? Lisa hates me, and my son isn't talking to me, either, at the moment. I'm afraid that I did behave rather badly."

Miriam looked genuinely distressed, and Josephine almost felt sorry for her. She knew what it was like to antagonize a child; she'd done it a time or two herself. But she'd had only her children's best interests at heart. And she was a mother, after all, which gave her the God-given license to interfere if necessary.

"How are your knees, Miriam?" Josephine asked.

"My knees? Why, I guess they're good. I play tennis and try to keep myself fit. Why?"

"Because you and that husband of yours need to get down on your knees and beg your son's forgiveness, and then my daughter's. You must not only admit you were wrong, but you must ask for their absolution and pray they give it."

She gasped. "Beg? I have never begged for anything in my life. And I doubt Rupert would do so. He's a very proud and stubborn man."

"Time to start, Miriam. You owe it to your future grandchild, and you owe it to Lisa. And as for your husband, I'm sure you have ways to convince him."

She arched a meaningful eyebrow and the woman blushed again.

"But what would I say to convince Lisa or Alex? I don't have a very good track record with either of them, I'm afraid."

"I would start with 'I'm sorry' and go from there."

Miriam took a moment to contemplate Josephine's words. Finally, she nodded. "You're a wise woman, Josephine Morelli, though a bit bossy, I must say. But I like your strength. Are you certain you're not from the South? We've got alligators in Florida with less tenacity."

Warming a little to her daughter's mother-in-law, even though the woman was affected and snobbish, Josephine replied, "Southern Italy, maybe. So, are you going to help me get Alex and Lisa back together? I can't do this alone."

"Yes, but if I do and this doesn't work out the way you want, you must promise not to send any of those Mafia people after me or my husband."

The Italian woman swallowed a smile. "Well, maybe just a horse head or two, but I promise nothing more than that."

ALEX WALKED INTO the Harley-Davidson store and felt totally conspicuous, like a duck out of water. Or maybe he was just *quacked!*

But if he wanted to win Lisa back, he would have to dress to impress her. It was painfully clear that she preferred the macho type to the Ivy League variety of male.

"Do you need some help?"

He turned at the sound of the woman's voice and his eyes widened as he took in the very well endowed, scantily dressed red-haired salesclerk. He supposed she was what everyone referred to as a "biker chick." She sure looked the part.

"Uh, yes. I'm looking for a leather jacket."

"And pants," she added, matter-of-factly. "You can't ride a Hog without leather pants, or you'll scorch your balls all to hell."

"Oh."

The young woman squinted at him. "You don't look much like a biker, if you don't mind my saying so. I don't mean to be insulting, but...well, bikers tend to have a certain look about them. Are you sure you wouldn't be interested in buying a Vespa instead?"

He sighed. "I'm not a biker. But my wife goes for that sort, so I'm—"

Her face lit up. "That's so sweet! My old man couldn't care less about what I like. And Zip couldn't fit his fat ass into a pair of leather pants if his life depended on it."

Lisa, Alex thought, *you had better appreciate this, that's all I've got to say.*

IN THE TWO WEEKS LISA had been working at Smollensky's Bakery, she thought she'd died and gone to Heaven. She loved everything about working with

Sol...well, with the exception of getting up at the crack of dawn. But the benefits definitely outweighed the drawbacks.

She was becoming quite proficient at cake decorating, and her lemon-meringue pie was to die for. Sol was a genius in the kitchen and, as a teacher, there was none better. He was patient and kind, and seemed to take genuine delight in sharing his knowledge and expertise. He and Lisa had grown as close as a favorite uncle and niece.

It was still early in the morning. They hadn't opened for business yet, and Lisa relished the time to get better acquainted with the older man.

"So how come you and Olivia never had any kids, Sol?" Lisa asked, rolling out a lump of dough for the pecan pies she was making.

"Olivia couldn't have kids. Female trouble, you know. We were content. But I know she would have loved to have a bunch of young ones underfoot. Olivia had a great capacity for love."

"I guess the bakery became her baby, huh?" Lisa certainly understood how that could happen. If she owned part of the business, she wouldn't want anything to interfere with making it a success.

Kids were highly overrated, anyway. At least, that's what she kept telling herself, since it seemed she wasn't likely to have any.

Come to think of it, men were even more highly overrated!

"She loved this place. Olivia was a real people person. I stayed in the back, for the most part, baking and taking care of the ordering, and she worked with the customers. It was her favorite part of the business."

"I like that part, too, though I really prefer the baking end of it. I feel a real sense of accomplishment when something I create with my own two hands turns out well and others like it. Mrs. Semolina complimented me on my oatmeal-raisin cookies the other day."

Sol grunted his disgust. "That old bag isn't easy to please, so you should feel proud of yourself. *I'm* proud of what you've learned in the short time you've been working here. Have you given any thought to baking for a living? You have the talent for it."

Rolling pin in hand, Lisa paused, pleased by the man's compliment, but knowing it wasn't possible. "I think about it all the time, Sol, but I don't have the money to start my own business.

"I've never had the self-confidence to make serious plans about anything. I've just sort of coasted through life, and then I met my husband. The rest, as they say, is history."

Or hysteria, depending on how you look at it.

"After you get divorced you might have some capital to invest, no?"

She shook her head. "I don't want anything from Alex. Even though he's well-off, I don't feel I'm entitled to any of his money. He's worked hard for it, and we weren't married long enough for me to stake a legitimate claim."

"You're an honest young woman. I like that about you."

Lisa smiled. "Honest but poor."

"You have a good heart. That is worth more than all the money in the world."

"Do you think my creditors will feel the same?" she quipped, winking at the older man, who smiled.

"I've been thinking about my future and this bakery, Lisa, and I've come to the conclusion that I like having you around. It's not so lonely when I have you to talk to. And it's making my burdens lighter that you're helping with the baking."

"Thanks, Sol! That's nice of you to say."

"Nice doesn't have anything to do with it. What would you think of coming to work here full-time?"

"Really?" Lisa's heart began pounding with excitement. Tossing aside the rolling pin, she threw herself at the older man, wrapping her floured hands around his thick waist. "I would love it. But are you sure? I'm not very experienced."

Sol chuckled. "Of course, I'm sure. What am I, senile? In time, if you continue to do well, we might talk of a partnership. But that's in the future. First, we must see how you do baking full-time. And you must be more tactful with the customers. You can't be telling the men who flirt with you to shove an éclair up their— well, you know."

"I'll try to be better." Lisa grew thoughtful for a moment, wondering what she was going to say to Leo and Francie, who had taken a big chance by giving her a job.

"I've got to give notice at work. I don't want to leave Leo and Francie shorthanded. I hope you understand."

"So you'll tell them and start here at the bakery as soon as you can. The job will still be here when you're ready."

"I don't know how to thank you. You don't know how much this means to me."

Sol chuckled. "I was young once, so I think I do." The bell over the door tinkled just then, and the older man added, "Here comes our first customer. Why don't you go out and sell him half of what we made this morning."

"I will. I'm so happy nothing and no one can ruin my day today."

But as Lisa stepped out to the front of the bakery and focused on the man in black leather, her smile disappeared and she almost choked on her words, not to mention the doughnut she was munching

9

"WHAT ARE YOU DOING HERE?" Lisa blurted out, forgetting her promise of moments before to be nice to the customers.

Surely there had to be exceptions.

And soon-to-be ex-husbands were definitely exceptions.

"I heard you were working here and came by to say hello. As I told you the last time we spoke, we need to talk about our future."

Lisa squinted as she tried to take in Alex's very unorthodox appearance. "Why are you dressed like a biker?" It was then she noticed the Harley parked outside the bakery, gleaming in the streetlights that lit the early-morning darkness, and her mouth fell open.

Alex riding a motorcycle? I don't think so.

"I hardly recognized you when you came in." He was dressed in a tight black T-shirt and even tighter blue jeans; a black-leather jacket completed the ensemble. His dark hair had been slicked back and he looked damn good...for a James Dean impersonator.

Alex wearing an earring! I don't think so.

ALEX SIGHED, WONDERING if he was ever going to get anywhere with his stubborn wife. He'd dressed like a macho jerk because he figured she was into that type of man. Her dance partners at the club had run to the chick-magnet type, so Alex figured if he couldn't beat 'em, he may as well join 'em.

His damn pants were so tight, he doubted he'd ever be able to sire children. But at least they weren't leather. He had drawn the line at that.

Well, if Lisa wouldn't respond to politeness, he knew how to remedy that. "Get your stuff! We're getting out of here. You're my wife, and I'm taking you with me. It's time you put aside all this nonsense, Lisa, and returned home. We have a life together, in case you've forgotten."

At his caveman antics, Lisa's eyes became the size of saucers. She stared at him as if he were deranged or from another planet. "Have you been drinking again?" She sniffed the air. "I'm not going anywhere with you, Alexander Mackenzie. Not now, not ever. When are you going to figure that out? We're through, finished. Stick a fork in it and call it done."

He winced at her ferocity. But Alex being Alex, and not one to take no for an answer, persisted. "You responded to my kiss the other night, and you know it. Admit it—you liked it. I know you're not as disinterested as you pretend to be. You still want me. We're good together, you and I."

"Get over yourself! And get out of here. This started out to be a very nice day, until you showed up."

"I'm not giving up, Lisa. We will be together. You love me. I know it, and you know it. So why are you being so damn pigheaded about it? I've already apologized about the way I treated you. What do you want me to do, grovel at your feet? I will if I have to."

"What I want is for you to leave. You're making a spectacle of yourself. Thank God there are no customers to see you."

It was then Alex spied an elderly gentleman holding a rolling pin in a threatening manner and knew that Lisa had a champion waiting in the wings. "I'll leave, but I'm coming back. I love you, I want you in my life, and I'll do whatever it takes to make that happen."

Heart twisting painfully in her chest, Lisa watched Alex storm out the door. It took him a few tries to get the motorcycle started, but then he sped away, as if Satan himself were on his heels. "Well, that's that, I guess."

So why does it hurt so much? It's what you wanted, after all.

Sol stepped forward, still holding the rolling pin and looking not at all convinced by her words. "I wouldn't be too sure about that, young lady. The boy looks determined. He loves you. I've never seen a man so willing to toss his pride away for the love of a woman. I'm not sure I would have done as much for Olivia, and I loved her like crazy."

Sighing wistfully, she shrugged. "Not everything is meant to be, Sol."

"That's true. But sometimes there is no fighting what is."

STILL REELING FROM her confrontation with Alex, Lisa paced the apartment, hoping Leo would be back soon from his late-afternoon jog.

Since he'd taken up with Bruce, Leo, the couch potato, had turned into the marathon man. He'd been running two miles a day for the past few weeks and hating every minute of it.

When Lisa heard the key turn in the lock, her stomach filled with butterflies, the lump in her throat swelling to uncomfortable proportions. Telling Leo she was going to quit would not be easy. In fact, Lisa wasn't quite sure how she was going to do it, though she'd rehearsed several speeches while waiting for him to put in an appearance.

"Hey, sweetie!" Leo greeted her with a toothy smile, wiping his forehead dramatically with the designer scarf draped around his neck. Even while exercising, the fastidious man liked to be fashionable.

"I stopped by Smollensky's a little while ago to see you, but Sol said you had left early. I hope you're feeling okay."

Lisa described Alex's visit.

"Ah, well that explains why there's an angry-looking biker sitting out in front of our apartment complex. I didn't recognize him as Alex, but I did notice the man was hot. Sort of a Russell Crowe type, oozing with sexuality, huh?"

Crossing to the window, Lisa looked out to find Alex sitting on his bike at the curb and groaned. She shook her head, wondering if her staid, conservative mortgage-banker husband had lost all of his marbles. This was definitely not Alexander Mackenzie behavior. "Something like that," she said finally.

"Someone should tell the poor guy that he's wearing his earring in the wrong ear. That is, unless your rejection of Alex has turned him to the dark side. In which case—"

Shaking her head, Lisa had to smile. "Alex is still very heterosexual, just unaware."

"Pity. So, are we going to Club Zero tonight? You promised to be my date this evening since Bruce is out of town visiting his mother. I swear, but that man is thoughtful. Sometimes the big ones surprise you."

Lisa wasn't touching that remark with a ten-foot pole. "I need to talk to you about something very important, Leo. I've made a life-altering decision, and you may not want to go clubbing with me after I tell you what it is."

"Uh-oh. Sounds like a chocolate-chip-cookie type of conversation to me. Do we have any?"

Like a hopeful puppy, Leo followed Lisa into the kitchen, where she procured a large Tupperware container of cookies and two glasses of cold milk.

"I told you when I moved in here that I could take care of your sugar addiction."

He bit into the cookie and made a contented sound. "So you did, sweetie. So tell me, what is this big decision of yours? Are you reconciling with Alex?"

She made a face. "Definitely not! This has nothing to do with Alex."

"Then what is it?"

Taking a deep breath, Lisa said, "As I've explained many times before, Leo, I love to bake more than anything else in this world." *Well, except for having sex, maybe.* "I'm good at it, and Sol thinks so, too. He's offered me a full-time job at the bakery, and I'm going to take it. It's what I've always wanted to do. I hope you'll be happy for me." She held her breath, waiting for his response.

Wiping the milk mustache from his mouth, Leo set down his glass, not bothering to hide his surprise. "Are you sure about this, Lisa? I've got plans for you at the store. You can do very well there, if you choose to stick it out."

"I don't want to sound ungrateful, because I'm not. I really appreciate your hiring me and giving me a chance to build up my self-confidence and job skills. And I've really enjoyed working with you and Francie. But being a designer is not my heart's desire. I want to bake."

"Well, based on the taste of these cookies, I think you've found your calling. If you want to bake, then you should. Life's too damn short to be unhappy in your work, Lisa. Though we'll hate to lose you, I understand completely."

"I intend to give you two weeks notice. Will that be enough?"

Leo shook his head. "Not necessary. Since business has picked up so dramatically, I've already placed an ad in the *Inquirer* for additional help. I intend to hire another designer, as well as an assistant for Francie. I start interviewing tomorrow, and I'm certain we'll be able to fill your position quickly."

Lisa nibbled her cookie, swallowing more milk and wishing she could avoid asking the next question, but knowing she must. "Do you want me to move out, since I won't be working for you any longer?"

"What? And give up my opportunity for freshly baked cakes, pies and cookies? Not on your life, sweetie. You can stay here as long as you like. I've gotten used to your slovenly ways and cheerful personality. I think I'd be lonely if you left."

Lisa heaved a sigh of relief, and a rush of love filled her heart for this kind man. "Thank you! You've been a good friend to me, and to Francie. We're lucky to have you in our lives."

"I know that, and the feeling is mutual. Now pass the cookies. That damn running has worked up an appetite." He held out his leg. "By the way, do you think my thighs look firmer?"

Lisa nodded, trying not to laugh at the earnest look on her friend's face. "Oh, definitely. Much firmer. Bruce is sure to be impressed."

"Oh, stuff Bruce! I've got my eye on the most adorable pair of black running shorts. They've got red lightning bolts running up the sides. *Très chic.*"

"Are you sure you're not into this exercise program of yours just for the clothes?"

Leo grinned. "But of course I am, sweetie. You don't

think I'd go to this much trouble for a man, do you? After all, it's very hard to mess with perfection."

MARCH HAD COME IN like a lion. It was pouring buckets outside as Lisa and Molly shared lunch.

"Who's that cute guy in the leather jacket that keeps staring at you? He looks very interested."

Molly kept gazing over her shoulder, and Lisa felt like kicking her friend in the leg under the table. They were having lunch at Simply Salads to celebrate Lisa's new full-time job at Smollensky's.

"Its just Alex. He's been following me around for days. I should have him arrested for stalking, but I don't have the heart."

Molly sighed. "I wish someone that good-looking would stalk me. I would never have recognized Alex if you hadn't told me who it was. The man looks yummy enough to eat. How you can resist him is beyond me."

Taking a bite of spinach salad, Lisa wondered the same thing. Her defenses were definitely weakening, not to mention that she hadn't had sex in what seemed like forever. "What's happening with you and Alan? I thought you liked him."

"I liked having sex with him. Alan's great in the sack. But other than that, he bores me. Alan is too wrapped up in Alan. He's shallow and full of himself."

That was true of most of the men Lisa had dated over the years. Seeing Alex in his new "macho man" image had made her realize just how stupid her choices in men had been. She'd gone for flash, not substance.

Alex had been different; there was no denying that. He didn't have a shallow, self-centered bone in his body. He didn't lie, criticize or hold his Ivy League education over her or anyone else's head. For all his money, he was down-to-earth and kind.

Alex was a real man, a caring man—which was why, she supposed, that she'd thrown caution to the wind and married him so quickly. Men like Alex didn't come along every day. She could see that clearly now.

Good Lord! Maybe she was growing up.

Her need to spite her parents, to draw attention to herself, to defy society and its rules and conventions had definitely waned.

And wouldn't Josephine and John be pleased about that?

Her parents had pretty much written her off, and she could hardly blame them for it. She'd pushed their buttons and gotten the logical response. But maybe if they had expected more of her, as they had with Francie, Lisa would have expected more of herself. Of course, it was always easier to blame someone else for her shortcomings. But she knew the fault was mostly her own.

"Earth to Lisa. Hello? Where are you? You haven't heard a word I've said. This is supposed to be a celebration, remember? Instead, I feel like I'm at a damn funeral. What gives?"

"Sorry. I've just been thinking about regrets and realized that I've been a real pain in the ass to my parents. It's a wonder they still love me." She sighed.

"Mine have pretty much given up on me," Molly

confessed. "They hate my vintage wardrobe, the men I date and the fact that I didn't follow in my father's footsteps, so to speak, and become a podiatrist."

Both girls let loose an *"ewwww"* at the same time.

"Can you imagine touching all those smelly feet?" the redhead asked, making a face of disgust. "Grosses me out, just to think about it."

Glancing at Alex out of the corner of her eye and remembering his penchant for sucking her toes, Lisa decided not to share that tidbit of information with her friend.

Alex looked over just then and their eyes caught. Smiling sexily, he winked, and Lisa's toes began to tingle; not to mention other various and sundry parts of her body.

"I've got to go, Molls. I'll explain later." She tossed down a twenty-dollar bill to cover her lunch and stood.

"But why? We're not done with our lunch yet."

"I've just got to, that's all. I'll call you later."

Taking a page from Leo's book, Lisa sprinted out of the restaurant, eager to put distance between her and her irresistible husband.

"HAVE YOU CALLED Alex or Lisa?" Josephine asked her coconspirator, Miriam, over the phone. "I haven't heard my daughter mention it, and I'm sure she would have. As you know, you are not her favorite person."

There was silence, then a long, drawn-out sigh. "I'm still not sure what to say. What if Lisa hangs up on me?"

Josephine rolled her eyes, even though the spineless woman couldn't see her. "Say you're sorry, and she won't hang up. My daughter was raised with better manners than that, Miriam, despite what you think. And when are you going to call Alex? Surely you're not afraid of talking to your own son."

"Tonight. I'll do it tonight."

"Good. There's a lot at stake. Lisa still hasn't gotten her period."

"You mean—"

"We could be grandmothers soon, so don't put this off. We need to shove those two in the right direction."

"All right. I'll do my part."

"See that you do, Miriam, or a horse's head in your bed is going to seem like child's play."

At the woman's sharp gasp, Josephine smiled and hung up the phone. Sometimes being Italian really came in handy, she decided.

"YOU CATCH ON QUICKLY." Sol praised Lisa's ability to make each cream puff uniform in size and shape. "It took my wife years to master these, and you've done it in a week. Cream puffs are tricky."

The compliment—one of many she'd received this past week—made Lisa grin. She was about to respond when the bell over the door tinkled and Francie walked in.

"Hey, Lisa! Hey, Mr. S! How's it going?"

"Your sister is a genius in the kitchen. I've got a nice crumb cake put away for you, Francie. I'll go get it."

"Nice man," Francie said, watching the older man disappear into the back room. "Sounds like Sol is quite impressed with you, Lisa. I guess you made the right decision, after all."

"I think he's just happy to have an extra pair of hands to help him."

"Don't sell yourself short. You do that all too frequently. You're good at baking, and the man is smart enough to know it. You should be proud of yourself. I know I am."

Uncomfortable with her sister's effusive praise, Lisa changed the subject. "How goes the baby making?"

"Well, the sex has been out of this world, but so far the stick hasn't turned color."

"Don't look so bummed. It hasn't been that long."

"How about you? Did you get your period?"

The fact that everyone in her family kept tabs on her menstrual cycle was a bit unnerving, not to mention, weird. "Nope. But I refuse to worry about it. The chances of my being pregnant are slim to none." Lisa wished she felt as confident as she sounded. But after so many weeks, she was starting to grow concerned. It would be just her luck to find out she was pregnant when things were starting to go so well with her career—and her marriage was on the skids.

Francie arched an eyebrow. "Mom doesn't think so. It's all she talks about these days."

"That's just Mom. But maybe she won't be so disappointed if you come up fat."

"A few more crumb cakes and that won't be a problem."

Sol came out and handed Francie the bakery box he was holding. Thanking him, she said, "I can feel the calories multiplying as I stand here. My feet are getting fatter."

The older man grinned. "Nothing I bake has any calories. I don't allow them. But everything your sister makes is loaded with them." Sol winked at the girls.

"I wish that were true." Francie paid for her purchase and turned to leave. Searching her purse for her car keys, she wasn't paying attention to where she was walking and ran smack-dab into the next customer who entered the store.

It was Alex.

"Oh! Sorry," she said, turning quickly to give her sister a commiserating smile and mouthed, "Good luck," before hurrying out the door.

Lisa groaned at the sight of her sexy husband, wondering how much longer she could hold out. Alex was slowly wearing down her resistance.

This past week she had received from him four-dozen pink roses, two autumn arrangements and a bouquet of carnations. Leo was complaining that the apartment smelled like a funeral home.

Alex had also left frequent messages on her voice mail and even hired a mariachi band to serenade her two nights ago. Unfortunately, Leo had gotten into the spirit of things and had joined the band out in the hallway, wearing only his boxer shorts.

Elderly Mrs. Conforti had called the police.

"Hi!" Alex said. "You're looking especially pretty today."

Garbed in white pants and an apron, Lisa thought she looked like a milkman, but was pleased by the compliment, nonetheless. "Thanks. What brings you in today? I really don't have time for another confrontation, Alex, and I don't think it's appropriate for you to keep coming to where I work. I'm trying to earn a living."

"I came by to see if you'd go out to dinner with me tonight, maybe swing by Club Zero for old time's sake. I want to be friends."

Alex was still garbed in his biker attire, and Lisa decided it was sweet that he'd gone to so much trouble to impress her, though she liked the older version of her husband much better than the new one.

Macho men were a dime a dozen; there was only one Alex.

Lisa knew she was weakening. Alex was slowly but surely wearing down her resolve. And, of course, there was the awful truth that she loved him, in spite of everything. That didn't mean she was going to be stupid and not keep her guard up. Fool me once, and all that. But, she figured, dinner couldn't hurt.

"I guess I could, as long as you don't expect too much to come of it. I wouldn't want you to get the wrong idea."

Though Lisa knew without a doubt that a strong spark still existed between them, she wanted to find out if Alex would truly accept her for what she was and not for what his family wanted her to be.

And she intended to do that tonight, one way or another.

10

"ARE YOU OUT OF YOUR MIND, Alex? Asking your soon-to-be ex-wife out on a date is not a very smart idea. I've tried to explain the facts of life to you concerning divorce, but you're not listening."

Bill Connors was wearing his lawyer's face, and though Alex appreciated his advice, knowing his heart was in the right place, he didn't appreciate Bill always talking about divorce. That word—that entire concept—was not in Alex's vocabulary.

"I told you, Bill, I have no intention of divorcing Lisa. And I'm doing everything humanly possible to try and convince her not to divorce me." Like praying. He wasn't a very religious man, but he prayed a lot these days.

Running agitated fingers through his sandy hair as he paced the living room of his apartment, Bill shook his head then ground to a halt in front of his friend. "Listen, Alex, I appreciate your feelings on this matter. But as a divorce attorney, I must inform you that you are weakening whatever case you might have against Lisa. The woman is not likely to change her mind, no matter how many dates she accepts. And you're going to be left holding the bag—an empty one, I might add."

"I canceled my appointment with Riggs Bank because you said there was something important you had to discuss with me this afternoon, Bill. I'm assuming it isn't my situation with Lisa, though I appreciate your concern."

Bill squeezed Alex's shoulder. "Afraid I have some rather bad news for you, buddy. Annie's decided that she wants to move in with me. I'm afraid you're going to have to make other living arrangements."

Alex hadn't been sure what sort of news to expect from his new roommate, but being evicted hadn't been at the top of the list. Of course, he knew it had to happen some day. Bill had been very generous about letting him bunk in with him these past few weeks, and Alex, no doubt, had overstayed his welcome. "I totally understand. Three's a crowd, always has been. I'm glad things are working out between you and Annie. She seems like a very nice girl."

A skeptical expression crossing his face, Bill shrugged. "I'm willing to give it a try, but I'm not going to hold my breath. Living together usually sounds the death knell for a relationship. Marriage is even worse.

"You know that law they have that puts you in prison if you commit three felonies—three strikes and you're out, so to speak. Works the same for marriage, in my opinion."

"It doesn't have to be that way."

Bill arched an eyebrow and leveled a knowing look at Alex, who insisted, "Well, it doesn't."

"Will you be able to find a place to live on such short notice? I'm sorry as hell about this, Alex. Obviously, it wasn't my idea. Women are so damn persnickety about things."

"Not a problem. I'll find a hotel and be out tonight."

"Tomorrow's soon enough. Annie's working and her flight back to the States won't be until tomorrow afternoon. She's in Paris, at the moment."

"Okay. That'll give me time to make arrangements. I hope you know how grateful I am for everything you've done, Bill. I never expected to be here this long. Guess I thought Lisa would fall right into my arms, once she saw me. Dumb, huh?"

His friend shook his head. "I sure as hell hope this works out for you, buddy, because I've never seen a man so in love with a woman before. I hope she's worth it. You deserve someone wonderful." In an uncharacteristic gesture, Bill grabbed Alex and hugged him.

"I'm going to miss you. Having you here has been like having a brother around. Monday night football won't be the same without you."

"Yeah, me, too."

They broke apart, red faced at having shared their feelings.

"If things don't work out with Lisa, I hope you'll call me. I won't charge you for any legal advice."

"I appreciate that. But after tonight, I'm hoping I won't need it."

"You're that certain she'll come back to you?"

"I'm not certain about anything. Lisa's as stubborn and willful as they come. But I've found a tenacity I didn't know I had, and I'm not about to give up. The stakes are too high."

AT THE KNOCK ON THE DOOR, Lisa sucked in her breath, smoothed down the red spandex dress that clung to her body like a second skin, adjusted her plunging neckline to reveal even more cleavage than she'd originally planned, and slid into her stiletto heels—shoes so torturous that she almost changed her mind about wearing them. But if she was going to put Alex through his paces tonight, Lisa needed to put her best foot forward, so to speak.

Opening the door, she greeted her husband with a smile and waited for him to react. His response surprised her, but didn't disappoint.

"Wow! You look incredible," he said. She thought she saw an agitated movement at the side of his cheek, but she couldn't be sure. To his credit, Alex refrained from saying anything judgmental about her appearance. In fact, his comments were quite the opposite.

"Love that dress. Is it new?"

Lisa fluffed her hair, licked her lips and smiled her most enticing smile, wondering what had prompted Alex's new outlook on provocative dressing. Then, noting the prominent bulge in his crotch that suddenly surfaced, she figured all men were universally horny creatures, no matter how much they protested.

"Thank you! It's so *hard* to remain on the cutting

edge of fashion these days. Leo helped me pick out this dress. He has such exquisite taste, don't you think?"

Actually, what Leo had said when he insisted she wear the outrageous dress was that, if Alex didn't salivate and fall to his knees upon seeing her, he wasn't any kind of a man.

Well, Alex hadn't fallen yet, but he was getting close. She could feel it.

Shifting uncomfortably from foot to foot, he said, "Remind me to thank Leo the next time I see him."

Alex's smile didn't quite reach his eyes, and Lisa almost laughed at the supreme effort he made to bite his tongue. "I will. Shall we go?"

DINNER, THOUGH DELICIOUS, was a torturous affair for Alex, but he was determined not to let his jealous anger get the better of him tonight.

The waiters at Chez Francois had spent most of the evening ogling his wife's cleavage shamelessly, hovering over their table, from aperitif to dessert, as if he were the president of the United States and Lisa, the first lady.

No diner in the annals of food service had ever been treated so solicitously.

"You'd think those waiters had never seen a beautiful woman before," he commented over their crème brûlée. "Mmm. This is delicious. How's yours?" He licked the creamy mixture off the spoon with his tongue, happy to see Lisa's eyes following the gesture.

"Men seem to have a problem with breasts," she

stated, in her usual forthright manner, shaking her head in disbelief. "I'm not sure why that's so, but I find it totally ridiculous."

"I hope you're not referring to me, because I don't have any problem. I like breasts very much," Alex replied with a rakish grin. "I'd be happy to demonstrate."

Lisa ignored the offer. "I mean, you'd think every woman in the world didn't have breasts, for heaven's sake! Men, too, for that matter. Yours just aren't as developed. Breasts are for feeding and nurturing children. I don't understand what the big deal is."

Big being the operative word, Alex thought, admiring the luscious mounds that overflowed the low neckline of his wife's dress and remembering how they felt in his hands and beneath his lips.

He shifted in his seat. "So I take it that you noticed the waiters' attention?"

"I noticed. I almost said something to the smarmy one with the mustache, but I decided not to give him the satisfaction. The French can be so pompous and arrogant. Good thing they know how to cook. It's their only saving grace."

"When breasts look like yours, love, a man is going to pay attention. It would be hard not to."

"That's very sweet. But I didn't think you liked cleavage. You used to tell me it wasn't seemly for a married woman to expose herself so...so..." She shrugged. "I can't remember exactly how you put it."

But Alex did remember the prudish remark, and his

face reddened. "I was wrong to have said that. You should show off your beauty. I'm proud of the way you look. I guess I just wanted to keep you all to myself."

"Just because a woman wears a low-cut dress and other men look at her, doesn't mean they get to touch the merchandise, Alex. It's just for show, and to make us feel like women."

"Well, there's no doubt you're all that."

A soft blush touched Lisa's cheeks. "Thank you again. I seem to be thanking you a lot this evening."

"Tell me something," he began, and her eyebrows rose in anticipation. "Why did you agree to go out with me tonight when you've done your best to avoid me these past few weeks?"

Sipping her espresso, Lisa pondered the question, and then replied, "Marriage might not be for us, Alex, but we can still be friends. It took me a while to come to that conclusion. We get along great when we're not married."

It wasn't the answer Alex wanted to hear, and he attempted to mask his hurt by quickly changing the subject. "My mother called the other night. She was asking about you. Mother actually sounded concerned, if you can believe that." In fact, his mother had been calling quite a bit lately, being solicitous, asking about Lisa, and he had no idea why.

Lisa stiffened in her seat, clearly annoyed at the mention of his mother. "I can't. She called me, too, but fortunately she got my voice mail."

"With mothers, there's no telling. They have their own reasons for doing things." But Miriam had a definite purpose, Alex was positive of that. He just wasn't sure what it was. His mother wasn't impulsive and didn't do things by the seat of her pants. Rather, she was clever, calculating and concise.

"That's true. My mom is a perfect example of that."

Alex smiled. "Can you imagine what it would be like if those two got together? The planet as we know it would be altered forever."

Lisa clutched her stomach. "The thought makes me extremely nauseous."

"Really? I hope it's not the food. I can take you home, if you're not feeling well."

"I'm feeling fine—great, in fact," she said, her eyebrows drawing together in puzzlement. "I'm just full.

"Are you ready to go?" she asked. "I want to get to the club before all the good tables are taken."

"Isn't your redheaded friend going to save us one?"

"Molly doesn't know that I'll be there with you tonight. I'm kinda hoping she doesn't show up."

"Why not? Are you embarrassed to be seen with me in public?"

Lisa flashed Alex an exasperated look. "Molly is a dear friend, but she asks too many questions."

"About us?"

"Yes."

"And you don't have the answers?"

Lisa grew thoughtful for a moment. "I'm still working on the answers."

Willing to take a *maybe* rather than a *no*, Alex nodded. "Then let's go. The music awaits."

LISA HAD FORGOTTEN how much fun Alex could be when he put his mind to it. Her husband was a great dancer, and in the hour since they'd been at the club they had danced to almost every song, from fast to slow to funky.

Molly hadn't put in an appearance as yet, much to Lisa's relief—explanations weren't something she had a lot of right now, and her friend would want to know why Lisa was on a date with the man she intended to divorce. A mutual friend, Cissy Timmerhorn, had confided that Molly was expected around eleven.

Alex sipped his scotch and smiled, clearly enjoying himself. "Are you having fun?"

Lisa nodded. "I'd almost forgotten what a great dancer you are. Have you been practicing?" she teased.

He reached for her hand. "I do other things great, too, if you'd care to take a stroll down memory lane."

Sipping her margarita, Lisa felt her face heat and gazed flirtatiously at her husband over the salted rim of her glass. "Can you have a night of sex with no strings attached?" She held her breath, waiting for his answer. She wanted to make love with Alex, but on her own terms.

He arched a disbelieving eyebrow. "Can you?"

Before she could answer, a familiar figure strolled up to their table and Lisa almost groaned aloud. It was

Guy Wilkes, also known as The Preacher, for the way he preyed on women.

Noting the angry snarl crossing her husband's lips, she placed her hand over his, which was now fisted, and whispered, "He's just a friend."

"Hey, babe! You're looking hot tonight. How about a dance?"

"No thanks, Guy. As you can see, I'm here with someone tonight."

The tall man glanced over at Alex and nearly dismissed him, until recognition lit his eyes. "I remember you. You're the ex-husband, right?"

"I'm not ex yet, so take a hike, preacher-man," Alex said, tossing back the remainder of his drink.

Guy ignored the request by turning his back on Alex. "Come on, babe. You know how much I like the slow ones. And we dance so well together."

Lisa sighed, hoping that by appeasing Guy he would leave her and Alex alone for the rest of the evening. She intended to tell him as much, once she was out of earshot of her husband. "Do you mind, Alex?"

"I guess not," he replied, and though she was relieved that he was being calm and sensible, she was almost disappointed by his lack of jealousy, as stupid as that sounded.

"Quit holding me so tightly, Guy," Lisa warned her partner in no uncertain terms once they were on the dance floor, trying to put some distance between them. "And if you grind your hips into me one more time,

I'm going to put you permanently out of commission. Is that clear?"

Guy grinned. "Crystal, babe. Crystal."

SEATED ALONE AT THE TABLE, Alex was doing his best to control his temper as he watched Lisa and Guy dance, but he wasn't doing a very good job of it.

Letting another man dance with the woman he loved ranked right up there with lending someone your toothbrush or underwear. It wasn't something he felt comfortable with. And that discomfort grew to major proportions when he saw Guy push his hips toward Lisa's and slide his hands over her butt.

Slamming his glass down on the table, Alex cursed. "That's it," he said. Other patrons nearby turned to look as he jumped to his feet.

Heading directly for the dancing couple, Alex paused before them and tapped Guy on the shoulder. "I'm cutting in."

The man shook his head. "I don't think so. I was here first, and I've taken possession now. Possession is nine-tenths of the law, don't forget."

Lisa's expression grew concerned as Alex's lips thinned. "Please, Guy, just back off," she urged. "It's Alex's turn now. And I'm nobody's possession, so quit the macho act. You're making a fool of yourself."

Guy drew her tighter to his chest. "I said we're dancing here. Get lost, ex-man."

Guy placed his hands on Lisa's butt again and drew

her into his crotch; she tried to pull back, in vain. But she did manage to kick him in the ankle.

"Let me go, you moron!"

It was at that precise moment that Alex tackled Guy to the ground, his elbow accidentally hitting the man's nose, which began bleeding profusely, the bright red blood dripping onto his pristine white shirt.

"I told you to let go of my wife, asshole!"

The two men began rolling around the floor, like a couple of adolescent teenagers, exchanging slaps and curses, totally ignoring Lisa, who was standing by helplessly, watching and wringing her hands.

Unable to stand it a moment longer, Lisa cried out, "Stop it, you two! Stop fighting!" rushing over to try and pull her jealous husband off Guy.

A woman screamed at the top of her lungs.

Someone yelled, "Call the police!"

But it was unnecessary. The police had already been summoned by the bartender, and were now heading in Alex and Guy's direction.

The cop pulled Lisa off of Alex. "Step aside, lady. You're in enough trouble as it is."

Her eyes widened. "But—"

"Break it up, you two!" the officer in charge demanded, grabbing hold of Alex and pulling him back, while Guy remained sprawled on the floor, bleeding like a stuck pig. The two men and Lisa were then handcuffed and escorted out the door.

"See what you've done, Alex? You've made me a

criminal, with your jealous ways and nasty temper,'' Lisa told him.

Noting his wife's fury, and the fact that she had blamed him for everything that had happened, Alex sighed. He'd met Lisa at Club Zero, and now it seemed he'd lost her here.

11

THE WORST PART of getting arrested, in Lisa's opinion, wasn't the handcuffs, the public humiliation of being hauled off to jail in front of a roomful of people, some of whom she knew, or even having to converse with cellmates who were hookers and drug addicts.

No, the worst part of the entire ordeal had been facing her parents when they'd come down to the police station to bail her and Alex out of jail.

Humiliation and mortification didn't even come close to explaining how she'd felt.

Now two hours later, they sat in the living room of the Morelli home—a decorator's nightmare, but a retro seventies lover's dream—watching Lisa's father pace the green shag-carpeted floor, a disappointed look on his face, while Josephine wrung her hands in distress and silently prayed to the Almighty.

"I hope you two understand the seriousness of the situation," John began, grinding to a halt in front of the silent couple and leveling a disgusted look at his daughter.

"I don't mind telling you, Lisa, that your mother and I were very embarrassed to find you and Alex in such a terrible situation and are once again disappointed by your behavior."

Disappointed! So what else was new?

John shook his head and heaved a deep sigh that Lisa thought had more to do with the lateness of the hour than anything else. Her father liked going to bed promptly at ten every night, and it was way past midnight.

"Hauled off to jail like common criminals," Josephine wailed, crossing herself. "*Dio!* What will the neighbors think? I won't be able to hold my head up in church this Sunday."

"I'm sure Father Scaletti will forgive you, Ma, if you put enough money in his collection plate."

"Lisa!" her father warned.

"When are you going to grow up, Lisa?" Josephine admonished. "And you, Alex," she pointed an accusing finger at her son-in-law. "I expected better of you. You're supposed to be the levelheaded one in this relationship. My daughter is a bit wild, but you—"

"I didn't do anything, Ma. It was Alex," Lisa tried to explain. "He became jealous because I was dancing with another man, even though—"

"And why were you dancing with another man?" her father wanted to know. "You're married, in case you've forgotten." He turned to Alex.

"And why are you letting my daughter dance with someone else? Is this the way they do it in Florida? Where I come from we protect our women. We don't let them run off with other men, carousing and doing

God only knows what. What kind of a husband allows that?"

Red faced, Alex replied, "I can assure you, Mr. Morelli, that I didn't want Lisa dancing with anyone but me. But as you know, your daughter is a bit headstrong and so—"

Lisa practically vaulted off the sofa, her face a mask of fury. "Oh, so now it's my fault? That's rich, and so typical of you, Alex. Just like it was my fault when your parents decided to attack me for no reason.

"Do you see, Ma? Do you see why I left him?"

Josephine threw up her hands. "Enough! Sit down, Lisa. This is getting us nowhere. It does no good to place blame. Now is the time to fix what is broken, not make new damage.

"I think you and Alex should move in here with me and your father. Maybe if you were living under the same roof, things could be worked out between you.

"And don't forget, there could be other reasons to make your marriage work."

"What other reasons?" Alex wanted to know, turning to stare at his wife, a questioning look on his face.

"Nothing. My mother isn't a rational woman, in case you haven't noticed."

"Maybe so," Josephine said, unwilling to give an inch. "But I still want you and Alex to move in with us. It's the sensible thing to do, not that you've ever been a sensible young woman, with all your crazy ideas and independent ways."

Lisa's eyes widened. "Live here, with you and Dad?"

She started laughing, almost hysterically. "You're not serious?"

I'd rather be deprived of sex and chocolate for the next ten years. Okay, maybe five. Well, definitely one.

"I'm very serious, Lisa. I think it would be good for you. Your father and I talked it over on our way to the police station, and we've agreed not to take sides in the matter. We just want you and your husband to have some time together, where you can work things out. Living like a normal married couple might help you do that."

Normal? There was nothing normal about the Morellis. Was her mother insane?

Well, duh!

"I'm willing to give it a try," Alex said, and Lisa flashed him an angry look.

"Well I'm not! I think it's a horrible idea." Though part of her wanted to say yes—the part that needed to punish Alex. It would serve him right to live with her family, after the hell he had put her through with his. The Morellis had turned dysfunction into an art form. She wouldn't bother to explain how her sweet, elderly grandmother read *Playgirl* and *Cosmo* when she thought no one was looking.

Lisa knew that her parents' interference would do more harm than good to a relationship that was already skating on thin ice.

Not that she wanted a relationship with Alex, mind you!

And she also knew that if she was going to achieve

independence, she had to start doing things on her own, like finding an apartment.

As much as she enjoyed living with Leo, Lisa needed her own space and to make her own way in the world.

Independence had become her new goal.

Getting hired at the bakery had been the first step. Now she needed to prove, not only to Alex, her parents and his, but to herself, that she was capable at succeeding at life.

No more running, hiding, being impulsive and unreliable. Lisa was writing a new autobiography of her life and she was calling it "The Big Do-Over!"

"LISA, THIS IS MIRIAM. Rupert and I have been very worried about you, and we'd like to..." There was a pause in the voice-mail message, as if the caller had to consider her options before going on. "We'd like to be friends and try to work out our differences."

As if being arrested wasn't enough punishment for one night, Lisa was forced to listen to another message from her mother-in-law when she arrived home that night.

Miriam sounded sickeningly sweet and oh so nice, and Lisa wondered what the woman was up to now. "I think not, Miriam," she replied to the machine. "But thanks for the offer."

Too much had happened for Lisa to just forgive and forget. But isn't that what she had done with Alex? Hadn't she sort of forgiven him by allowing them to be friends?

It didn't seem conceivable, but could she do the same with her in-laws after everything that had happened?

And the real question was: Did she want to?

"SOL, I THINK WE NEED to implement a few changes around here. Though the bakery goods are by far the best in the city, we're not attracting a young enough clientele. We need a new name for the bakery, something with a bit more pizzazz. And we need to spruce the place up a bit, make it more trendy if we're going to compete with the likes of Starbucks."

Lisa held her breath, hoping Sol wouldn't take offense to the suggestions she'd been contemplating for days. But if the bakery was going to succeed against the stiff competition they faced, changes had to be implemented.

The owner of Smollensky's winced a few times as Lisa spoke of changing his beloved bakery, but he didn't throw the rolling pin he held at her, so Lisa took that as a good sign. She'd been working at the bakery almost a month, so she felt she had a right to speak her mind.

Of course, Lisa always felt she had a right to speak her mind.

"We have tradition here, Lisa. We're known in the neighborhood as a family bakery. What would my regular customers think if suddenly everything they are familiar with changes? They might not be willing to buy from me anymore. Old people don't like change, including me."

"I'm sure they'd be delighted. But it's the younger coffee-drinking crowd with the disposable income that we need to attract, Sol. They're the ones with the bucks."

She pointed at the piecrust. "We could call the bakery Rolling in the Dough. Sort of a double meaning, if you know what I'm saying."

He thought a moment. "Not bad. It's catchy. Olivia always thought we needed a different name for the bakery. She thought Smollensky sounded too Jewish and might not bring in the Catholics. Fortunately, that didn't happen. People know quality when they taste it."

Now that she'd gotten his attention, Lisa pressed her case. "I thought we could take down those old-fashioned lace curtains and put up some wooden blinds instead, maybe paint the walls a nice cream color and accent with a deep red. We could buy a few used tables and chairs and paint them to match. And if we served a variety of coffees and teas, we might sell more doughnuts, muffins and croissants in the morning, which would maximize profits."

Sol rubbed his chin, contemplating Lisa's argument for improving the bakery. "I like your ideas. Sounds to me like you put a lot of thought into them, and that's good. You have a good head for business, young lady." The older man winked at her.

"We could rip up this old carpeting," he added.

"There's a nice oak floor beneath it that we could refinish. Olivia thought it was too much trouble to take care of, so we carpeted over it."

Lisa was so excited that Sol was enthusiastic about her ideas she was practically jumping up and down. "It's going to look fantastic, Sol. We can have a grand reopening and get some press. I'll have Francie do it. She used to be a publicist and will know exactly who to call."

"It's going to cost, but I got a cousin who does remodeling work and he owes me a favor. I'll call Herman tonight and see what he says."

"And I'll get Leo to do the blinds and help with the decorating, at cost, of course. I'm sure he'd be willing. All you have to do is feed Leo sweets and he'll do anything."

"This is good, Lisa. I feel my old energy coming back. You have been good for this place, and for me."

Lisa hugged the portly man. "You've been good for me, too, Sol. For the first time in my life, I don't feel like a screwup. I feel needed, like I belong."

"You're a nice girl and a hard worker. We make a good team."

Beaming from ear to ear, she said, "This calls for a toast, and at least three chocolate-chip cookies."

Sol procured two bottles of water from the refrigerator and a tray of freshly baked cookies. "I just took these out of the oven."

As the gooey chocolate melted in her mouth, Lisa

heaved a contented sigh. "Eat your heart out, Mrs. Fields."

"You could be like her one day, Lisa. You have vision. That's what it takes to be successful. And being young and energetic doesn't hurt, either."

She paused midbite. "Do you really think so, Sol? I've never had such high aspirations."

"In this day and age a woman can do anything. What's to stop you?"

Lisa thought that over and nodded in agreement. "You're right. I can do anything I put my mind to."

Funny that Alex's image kept popping into her head.

LATER THAT SAME DAY, Alex moved in with the Morellis. He needed a place to stay, they had offered, and he wasn't one to look a gift horse in the mouth.

"I appreciate your putting me up, Mrs. Morelli. Your offer came at a good time, since my friend wasn't able to accommodate me at his apartment any longer."

Josephine led Alex into the spare bedroom, which was sparsely furnished with a twin bed, nightstand and not much else, but looked clean and comfortable, nonetheless.

"To be honest, I was hoping my daughter would come home, too. But it will be nice having you here, Alex. It will give us a chance to become better acquainted, and maybe Lisa will come around.

"She's a hard one, my Lisa. But I know in time she will listen to her heart and not her head. There's too much at stake."

"You mean our marriage?" he asked, tossing his leather carry-on onto the bed and winning a frown from his mother-in-law, who shook her head in chastisement.

"We don't dirty the bedspreads with luggage and we don't put our feet on the furniture, either," she said.

Alex promptly removed the offending item and apologized.

"Your marriage needs to be repaired, of course. But there are other factors to be considered, too. I'm sure you must realize that when two people are married certain *things* can result."

Alex thought a moment, and then all color drained from his face. "Are you saying that Lisa is pregnant?" That was one possibility he hadn't even considered. He'd just assumed because he had used condoms when they'd made love that pregnancy wouldn't be an issue. But condoms weren't foolproof, and he knew that.

Though he loved kids, Alex didn't think he or Lisa was ready for them yet. They had a marriage to repair, he had a business to get off the ground, and it was clear Lisa didn't know what she wanted from life. Of course, babies had a way of disregarding the best-laid plans of newlyweds.

Josephine shrugged. "That's not for me to say. My daughter won't admit to anything. But as a woman, I know the possibility exists. So I have taken it upon myself to contact your mother, Alex. I felt Miriam should be made aware of what is going on."

"My mother! You spoke to my mother? When?" This was news to him—very unwelcome news.

"Miriam came here to see me, not long ago, at my invitation. We had a nice chat about our children's future and the possibility of a grandchild. Your mother agrees that we must preserve your marriage to Lisa, at all costs."

Now that was a switch, and all because of a possibility of a grandchild. Alex tried to keep his temper in check, but he could feel the blood rising hot to his cheeks. "You and my mother should not have involved yourself in this, Mrs. Morelli. Child or no, what happens between Lisa and myself is our business."

Josephine looked hurt and confused. "But you came to me for help, asked my advice. Don't you remember?"

Heaving a sigh, Alex nodded. "Yes. Because I was at my wit's end." *And stupid, apparently.* "But by involving my mother, you have made the situation worse. Lisa and my family don't get along. That is what caused all of this trouble to begin with."

"Then that will have to be resolved, won't it? Rude or not, they are your parents, Lisa is your wife, and they need to fix their relationship. I told your mother as much."

Alex could only imagine how that conversation must have gone. Miriam Mackenzie did not like being told what to do by anyone, especially someone she considered a social inferior. *I-talians,* as she called them, were foreigners, in his mother's opinion, whether or not they'd been born in the good old U.S.A.

"I think it would be better if you kept this information to yourself, Mrs. Morelli, and not tell Lisa about talking to my mother. She's still quite angry with my parents and will not welcome any interference from them. In fact, I'm not sure she would even consent to see them, if the situation presented itself." And he hoped it wouldn't, anytime soon. But what were the chances of that, now that Josephine had gotten involved?

"I haven't said a word, not even to my husband. I thought it'd be better if Lisa believed your parents are being kind to her of their accord and not because of what I told your mother."

Alex scratched his head, beginning to see how manipulative both Josephine and his mother were. And why both sets of parents drove his wife nuts. They were beginning to have that same effect on him.

If Lisa came back to him, he would never allow his family or hers to interfere in their lives again.

"Even though I appreciate your trying to help, Mrs. Morelli, I need to think this new development through, and I'd appreciate it if you would not meddle again."

"Hmph! That's some appreciation I get for trying to help you, Alex. I thought you would be grateful. But children are never grateful to their parents, no matter how hard we try to help them."

She raised her hands heavenward. "I pray the good

Lord takes me soon, so I won't be such a burden to my family."

As Alex shut the door to his room, he could still hear Lisa's mother mumbling to herself about ungrateful son-in-laws and her impending death, and fully expected to be evicted from the premises by nightfall.

Which, come to think about it, might not be such a bad fate.

TWO DAYS LATER, LISA was in the kitchen, preparing a celebratory dinner for herself and Leo, who had purchased a standing rib roast in honor of her newly found independence. And only slightly ecstatic because Lisa intended to move into an apartment of her own, as soon as she could locate something suitable and close to the bakery.

Checking the roast one more time, she wiped her hands on the apron around her waist and began paring the potatoes to mash when a knock sounded at the door. She half hoped it was Alex, whom she hadn't seen since he'd moved in with her parents. She was dying to know how he was faring. The thought of her mother bossing him around had her smiling evilly as she hurried to answer the summons.

Lisa wasn't prepared for the sight that greeted her.

Miriam and Rupert Mackenzie stood on the other side, holding a bouquet of daffodils and carnations. Alex's mother smiled, handing her the flowers, which Lisa crushed to her chest, as if they could protect her from the enemy.

"Hello, Lisa. May we come in? We won't take up much of your time."

A multitude of emotions surged through Lisa, one of which was anger at their audacity in just showing up on her doorstep, as if she had nothing better to do than entertain them. "That's good, because I'm preparing dinner for a guest." She placed the flowers on the sideboard, unwilling to give them too much attention, lest the Mackenzies thought she could be bought off so easily.

"Is my son coming over for dinner? I'd like to speak to Alex," Rupert said, looking vastly uncomfortable at being in her presence, as he shifted from foot to foot.

It was clear to Lisa that it was not his idea to be here.

"No, he's not. Alex is living with my parents, for the time being, so you might want to visit him over there."

"Oh?" Miriam was clearly surprised. "We will, but we'd like to talk to you first, if that's okay."

Lisa wasn't sure she wanted to speak to the Mackenzies after all they had put her through, but she was determined not to be as rude as they were. "I didn't think we had much to say to each other. Am I wrong?" she asked, inviting them to sit on the sofa.

"What a lovely room," Miriam remarked, her gaze touching on all the fine antiques and beautiful fabrics that were Leo's pride and joy.

"We came here in person to apologize. Leaving phone messages is just not adequate, I'm afraid.

"Rupert and I realize that we were not as welcoming as we should have been when you came to live with us, and feel badly that we have caused a rift between you and Alex. Please forgive us."

Lisa was so stunned at that point you could have knocked her over with a feather.

Miriam Mackenzie apologizing? Would wonders never cease?

After she found her voice, she said, "I'm not sure I will ever forgive you," and noted how Alex's father winced. "But I do accept your apology and appreciate your courage in giving it."

"My son is a peacemaker," Rupert said. "Always has been. I think what you perceived as Alex taking our side, was merely his way of trying to make peace, while keeping the family together. We were wrong to put him in that position."

"Yes, we were. I hope in time you will find it in your heart to forgive us, Lisa, and we hope Alex will, too," Miriam said. "He's still very angry with us, and rightly so."

Lisa wondered if this was some alien creature dressed up to look like Miriam, because this person certainly didn't sound or act like the Miriam Mackenzie she knew. That woman would never have eaten humble pie.

"We want you to know that you are welcome in our family, and that if you do decide to come back, we will endeavor to make up for our previous rudeness and inhospitality."

"Warts and all?" Lisa couldn't help asking, arching an eyebrow. "It seems you weren't too happy with the way I dressed, talked and behaved. Are you sure you want me around your friends? I didn't get that impression, especially when it came to the country-club crowd."

"Friends are friends, but family is what's important."

Before Lisa could respond to Miriam's remark, the door opened and Leo came strolling in, carrying a bottle of wine and wearing a burgundy-velvet suit, along with a big smile.

"I dressed up for the occasion, sweetie."

Alex's parents stared first at Leo, eyes widening at his flamboyant appearance, and then at Lisa, for an explanation.

"Oh, sorry. I didn't realize you had company," Leo said.

"This is Leo Bergmann, my roommate. Leo's gay, in case you were thinking that something's been going on between us," Lisa told her in-laws, quite matter-of-factly.

Miriam's and Rupert's eyes widened at that disclosure, but remained silent.

"Leo, this is Miriam and Rupert Mackenzie—Alex's parents."

Leo stuck out his hand to Rupert, who finally gave his after thoughtful consideration, as if homosexuality might be contagious. "Pleased to meet you. I've heard oodles about you two," he said, smiling at Miriam, who nodded curtly in return.

The Mackenzies rose to their feet. "We hope you'll

take to heart what we've said, Lisa." Miriam smiled encouragingly. "It was nice meeting you, Mr. Bergmann." With that, she and her husband hurried out of the apartment.

Once the door closed behind them, Lisa burst out laughing. "I don't think they've ever met a gay man before."

"At least not one whom they knew was gay," Leo agreed. "Why did they come here? Did they try to pay you off, ask you not to see Alex ever again?"

Lisa shook her head. "They came to apologize, if you can believe that. I certainly can't. It's so strange. I don't think it was Alex's idea, either. They haven't seen him yet, from what I was led to believe."

"So why the change of heart?"

She shrugged. "Beats me. But they want to welcome me back to the family fold."

"Yeah, so they can smother you."

"I don't know." Lisa grew contemplative. "They seemed very sincere."

And if she could get along with Alex's family, then maybe...

"I thought we were going to celebrate your independence," Leo reminded her. "Are you seriously thinking about giving up your job at the bakery and moving back to Florida to live? Would you be happy there, after how hard you've worked to become liberated?"

Lisa shook her head, unable to answer. She hadn't thought that far. And even if she had, she didn't have the answers to any of the questions floating through Leo's mind, or hers.

12

ALEX AND LISA ENTERED the movie theater the following evening at eight o'clock, loaded down with popcorn, Milk Duds and soft drinks.

Once they were seated inside the nearly empty cinema, Alex turned to Lisa and said, "I appreciate your going out with me tonight. Hell, after my parents impromptu visit of yesterday, I wasn't sure if you'd still be talking to me." He'd been furious when he'd found out what they'd done. But by then, of course, it had been too late. Miriam and Rupert had proceeded, as usual, with no thought to anyone else's wishes.

"I take it you had no idea that your parents were in town," Lisa replied, reaching over to grab a handful of the buttery popcorn and stuffing it into her mouth. She made appreciative noises that had Alex's gut tightening.

He cleared his throat. "None whatsoever. I haven't had any contact with either of them since shortly after you left Florida. And then they just show up on your parents' doorstep, unannounced, like it was the most natural thing in the world for them to be there." He wouldn't bother to mention that Josephine had probably initiated the visit. He'd bet money on it, in fact.

"How did my mom react? She's not overly fond of your mother and father, you know. She compares them to Mussolini."

Alex smiled at the comparison. "Josephine was gracious and invited them in for coffee and dessert. They didn't stay long. Just long enough to beg me to come home, remind me of my familial duties, etcetera, etcetera."

"And how did you hold up during all that? I'm sure it must have been difficult. Your parents are not the type of people to pull any punches. They certainly didn't with me."

"Okay, I guess. It was awkward at first, seeing them after such a long time with no contact, but we made the best of it. They're my parents. I love them. What else could I do?"

"Nothing, I guess. Did they say why they haven't tried to reach you?"

"My dad said he tried calling me on my cell phone several times, to tell me he wants me back working in his firm. I said no. I'm determined to make a go of this new venture, no matter what I have to do. It's time I became self-reliant. I should have done it years ago."

Hindsight was always twenty-twenty, unfortunately.

Alex's feelings regarding his future seemed to reflect Lisa's pretty closely, and she acted pleased by his response. "So how's it going? Mom told me that you were starting your own mortgage company. That seems like a pretty ambitious undertaking."

"Trying to. I've been meeting with bankers, investors, insurance companies, getting my ducks in a row. My last name has opened a few doors, but I'm determined to do this on my own. It won't be easy, and there's a lot of risk involved—not to mention money—but I think I can do it."

"Will you have to borrow a lot to get started? I doubt your parents will give you any, under the present circumstances."

"I wouldn't take it, even if they would. When my grandmother died she left me a small inheritance, which I intend to invest in the company."

"I'm sure you'll be every bit as successful as your dad."

Alex felt a warm glow. "That's nice of you to say. I learned a lot from working with my father. He's a smart businessman, for all his failings as a human being. But I don't want to run my business like he does, with no heart, thinking the only important thing is the bottom line. I want to treat people with dignity and respect. I want to help them succeed."

"Pardon me for saying so, Alex, but you're nothing like your father. And that's a compliment."

"Thanks. I know if given the chance, I can be successful at running my own mortgage business."

"Sometimes all we need is a chance," Lisa said meaningfully, and Alex nodded, wishing again that he hadn't been so blind and stupid where his wife had been concerned. For a smart guy, he'd been pretty damn dumb.

"Guess you weren't given much of a chance by my folks. I'm sorry about that. You deserved better."

"They've apologized and I've accepted."

"That was gracious of you, considering everything they put you through."

"I said I accepted their apology, not that I've forgiven them, Alex. That will take some time, if ever."

"I'm a patient man. I'll wait however long it takes you to forgive me. I pray only that you will." He squeezed her hand. "I love you. Always have, always will."

Lisa sighed. "Oh, Alex. Everything's such a mess. How did we get to this place? I really thought—" She shook her head. "Never mind."

"What? Tell me."

"That I'd found what I was looking for in a man, that for the first time in my life I had tossed aside all my preconceived notions and let my heart rule my head. But I see now I was wrong to do that. We're just too different people from too different worlds. Our marriage would never have worked, even if your parents hadn't interfered."

"That's not true! Okay, so we're different. So what? That's what makes life interesting. I admit, I was an ass for not standing up for you with my parents. But I love you, Lisa, and I want us to be a couple again. I'll do whatever it takes to make that happen."

The theater darkened and Lisa lowered her voice to a whisper as the previews began to play. "I have a lot to think about, Alex, things to sort out about what I truly want. Now is not the time for that. I won't be able to concentrate with Kevin Costner on the screen."

Her attempt at levity made him smile. "Hard to compete with a cowboy, I guess."

"Yep. And Kevin plays one so well."

"Costner just acts like himself. Not much real acting going on, if you ask me."

"Yeah? Well, so did John Wayne and he became a Hollywood icon. Not bad for a cowboy, huh?"

Alex sighed, willing to accept defeat. "It's doubtful I'm going to win this argument, so I'll just keep my mouth shut. Pass the popcorn."

"HEARD YOU AND ALEX had a date last night. What's up with that?"

Tucking her feet beneath her, as she made herself more comfortable on Leo's sofa, Francie reached for the glass of milk her sister had placed on the coffee table.

"There was no necking in the balcony, if that's what you're asking," Lisa tossed back, reaching for an oatmeal-raisin cookie before sitting down beside her.

She would love to have swapped spit with Alex, but that wouldn't have been a very smart idea, as confused as she was at the moment.

"Mom thought it was a big enough deal to tell me about. I was just curious, that's all."

Lisa sighed. "Alex spent a good portion of the evening apologizing. We discussed our differences, which he totally discounted. He seems to be pulling away from the hold his father had over him, and is starting his own mortgage-banking business."

"But that's good, isn't it?"

"I guess."

"You know you love him, Lisa. Most of us get only one shot at true love, and I think you've found yours with Alex."

"I do love Alex. I always have, I guess."

Francie looked inordinately pleased by the confession. "So, are you getting back together? I really hope you do, Lisa. I've given your situation a lot of thought, and I've come to the conclusion that you and Alex belong together. It wouldn't be fair to the baby not to have two parents to—".

"Whoa!" Wide-eyed, Lisa held up her hand. "What baby? What on earth are you talking about?"

"I told you that Mom is positive you're pregnant, and she's been telling that to everyone who will listen. I just assumed—"

"Who's everyone?"

"The Mackenzies, for starters. They are overjoyed at the prospect of becoming grandparents, according to Mom."

Nearly choking on the cookie, Lisa grabbed the milk glass out of Francie's hand and swallowed a large gulp. "Dammit! No wonder they were so apologetic and nicey nice when they came by here the other day. I had a feeling something was up. I just wasn't sure what."

And if the Mackenzies knew, then Alex surely knew. But he hadn't let on or said a word.

Was the idea of a baby the reason he'd been pushing so hard to reconcile?

"Mom likes the Mackenzies. She says once you get to know them, they're not bad people."

"Yeah, I'm sure that was true of Mussolini, too. Well, hooray for Mom. Maybe she can move in with them."

"Don't get mad at me. I'm just telling you what she told me. So, are you pregnant? Do you know for sure one way or the other?"

"All the home pregnancy tests I've done have come back negative. But I still haven't gotten my period."

"Those tests aren't foolproof, Lisa. You could still be pregnant. You should go see a doctor, get a professional opinion. At least you would know, once and for all."

"You mean that I shouldn't just take Mom's word for it, like everyone else?"

And what would she do if she found out she was pregnant?

A baby wasn't a good enough reason to stay in a marriage. There had to be love, respect, trust and all that other stuff the minister had mentioned.

And she did love, respect and trust Alex, but was that enough to overcome the differences between them?

Her sister shrugged. "Mom made a pretty convincing argument, Lisa."

"What about you? Is the stork about to visit your house?"

Hemming and hawing, Francie said finally, "I'm not certain. I've had inconclusive results—two have been positive and two have been negative. I have an appointment with Dr. Franklin in a couple of weeks."

"Really?" Lisa's eyes lit with excitement. "And do you think you might be?"

"I don't want to get my hopes up. I may just be trying to convince myself I am because I want to have a baby so badly. Mark thinks we should just wait and see what the doctor says. We're not telling anyone about this, including Mom and Dad, so you are sworn to secrecy."

"If I know you, Francie, you've already dragged Mark to the baby store to look at cribs and baby furniture."

"Just once." She sighed. "I've been praying every night."

"I'm sure it'll all turn out the way you want it to."

"And how do you want things to turn out for you, Lisa?" Francie asked. "You love Alex, and he loves you. But now that you've got that great job at the bakery and all those plans in the works, are you going to be able to just give them up and go back to your idle, rich life in Florida?"

"I would never go back there, and Alex knows it. We haven't discussed anything like that yet, but I've made my feelings pretty clear on the subject of family interference. And I think Alex is getting a large dose of that by living with Mom, the world's master manipulator. He told me she's been giving him instructions on the proper way to do his laundry." Lisa grinned, and Francie laughed aloud.

The words were no sooner out of Lisa's mouth when the phone rang. She answered the portable and groaned.

"Lisa, it's your mother. Are you taking care of yourself, drinking plenty of milk? I heard about the refurbishing of the bakery and I don't want you breathing in those paint fumes. It's not good for the baby."

Lisa counted to ten beneath her breath, asked God for patience, and then said, "What baby is that, Mom? Have you been spreading false rumors about me?"

"Of course not! I'm just telling people about the possibility that you could be carrying Alex's child."

"And I hear that you told this to Alex's parents. Is that true?"

A long silence, then, "I may have mentioned something to the Mackenzies about it. As the grandparents, they have a right to know."

"There is no baby. I keep telling you that. I don't appreciate you getting their hopes up about something that isn't going to happen."

"You can't be certain of that. You haven't been to the doctor yet."

"I think I know my own body, Ma. I've been telling you I have no symptoms. I'm not throwing up, my boobs aren't sore or any bigger, and I haven't gained an ounce since I've been back."

"I should hate you for that," Francie called out, making a face at Lisa, who grinned and rolled her eyes.

"Is your sister there? Is that who you're talking to? You girls have plenty of time for each other, but no time to visit an elderly lady who could die at any moment."

Lisa sucked in her breath. "Is Grandma ill?"

Josephine cursed in Italian. "No. I was talking about myself. You never know how long I'll be around."

"You'd probably be around a lot longer if you'd quit asking God to take you every day," she replied, breathing a deep sigh of relief that her grandmother was okay. "One of these days He's going to get tired of your asking and just do it." Lisa could picture Josephine crossing herself.

"You and that husband of yours deserve each other. Alex told me not to butt into your lives, and now you are being rude to me, as well. I'm very hurt."

"Alex told you not to interfere?" Lisa was surprised, and thrilled.

"Yes. And you needn't sound so happy about it. All I did was inform Miriam about the baby and he became quite upset and very vocal about it."

"Maybe there's hope for Alex after all."

"What's that supposed to mean? You want him to be rude to your mother? What kind of a daughter wants that?"

Lisa sighed. "Listen, Mom, Francie and I love you. But we don't want you meddling in our lives. We're grown women. We're both married and have our own lives to live."

"Hmph! And not without my help. You just ask your sister about that. Without me, she wouldn't be married now."

"I'm sure Francie is eternally grateful that you dragged her to the altar on four different occasions, Mom."

Hearing that, Francie clutched her stomach and made gagging sounds.

"Why is your sister laughing? Does she know how much money those weddings cost us?"

Unwilling to venture down a road that had been traveled many times before, Lisa thought quickly. "Leo's home, Mom," she lied. "I gotta go. I'll come by and see you tomorrow, bring you a crumb cake, after I'm done at the bakery."

Josephine uttered a few more choice words in Italian, and then finally hung up, much to Lisa's relief.

"That was fun."

"Better you than me," Francie said. "Mom's been driving Mark and I crazy about giving her grandchildren. She even threatened to come over and show Mark what he was doing wrong."

Lisa, who could well imagine her mother saying that, burst into giggles. "What did Mark say?"

"That the bed wasn't large enough for three, but thanks anyway."

"And how did Mom respond to that?"

"I don't know. She hasn't spoken to Mark since. I think she's still mad at him."

"Lucky Mark," Lisa said, sighing wistfully.

BRIGHT AND EARLY the next morning, Lisa entered the bakery, which was temporarily closed for renovation, and was quite surprised to find Sol having coffee with Alex. They were chatting like old friends.

Alex was dressed for manual labor in jeans and a T-shirt. It wasn't his Harley look, thank goodness, but it was definitely his hunky one. He looked as yummy as a chocolate-glazed doughnut.

And Lisa was very fond of chocolate-glazed doughnuts!

"Alex, what are you doing here?"

He smiled. "I've come to help with the painting and anything else you might need me to do. Sol says he wants to reopen the bakery next week, so I figured you two could use an extra pair of hands."

Her jaw dropped. "But how did you know we were remodeling? I'm positive that I didn't mention it."

"Leo told me. By the way, he said to tell you that he'd be by later to measure the windows for the blinds."

"What am I, chopped liver, that you don't say good morning?" Sol chastised Lisa with a wink.

She hurried over to the table where the man was seated. "I'm sorry, Sol. I was just surprised to see Alex here, that's all."

"So I noticed. Well, we can certainly use the extra

help. I hate painting. Olivia had to bribe me to paint and wallpaper." Sol's eyes were twinkling with merriment. "I won't tell you what she used for incentives."

Alex laughed, and Lisa very uncharacteristically blushed. "Oh," was all she could think to say.

Francie and Mark showed up shortly after that, and then Leo and Bruce strolled in.

"Hey, sweetie!" Leo called out. "Make way for the gay contingent," he said, swishing his hips in an exaggerated manner that even had conservative Sol laughing.

At that moment, Lisa felt truly blessed. Her family and friends had come to help her turn her ideas for the bakery into a reality. And her husband, the man she was still madly in love with, was here for her, too, just as he'd always been. She had just been too immature and emotionally insecure to see that before.

Lisa realized that what she had perceived as weakness in Alex was in reality compassion and caring for his parents. She could see quite clearly now that he'd been torn between his need to placate them and keep peace in the family, and his desire and love for her.

And she hadn't made it easy on him. Just as she'd never made it any easier on her own family when she'd rebelled against every suggestion and opinion they'd given—out of love for her, and to help her understand that she wasn't the center of the universe, that the world did not revolve solely around her wants and needs.

It was a humbling realization, and she was much wiser for finally figuring it out.

Picking up a paintbrush, she headed across the room in her husband's direction, hoping to repair more than just the bakery.

13

TO THANK ALEX for his help at the bakery these past few days, and to finally discuss the state of their marriage, such as it was, Lisa had invited him over for dinner, and he was due to arrive at any moment.

This time, she had dressed primly for the occasion, in a long-sleeved black knit dress, accessorized with faux pearls and small dangling earrings, to prove that she could be the kind of wife Alex needed—conservative, composed, caring. She had prepared his favorite dinner of garlic bread, salad and lasagna, which she'd been slaving over since early in the morning.

Her sauce wasn't quite as good as her mother's, but Lisa thought it would pass muster with a non-Italian, white-bread boy from Florida, who'd been eating fast food most evenings—Josephine had decided not to cook for a son-in-law she deemed ungrateful—and therefore couldn't be all that choosy.

Leo had gone into New York City to meet old friends and attend the theater, so she and Alex would have the apartment all to themselves tonight, not that it would do them any good.

The lovemaking gods were apparently not pleased with her at the moment.

After almost twelve weeks of uncertainty, Lisa had gotten her period last night.

Which was disappointing, as far as making love to her husband was concerned—something she desperately wanted to do—but good for her peace of mind. Not being pregnant was one less complication in a marriage already fraught with complications, so maybe the lovemaking gods weren't so mean-spirited, after all.

Having your period was like having a built-in chastity belt, unless you were the red-badge-of-courage type, who just went for it, no matter what, but that wasn't Lisa's cup of tea.

The doorbell rang and Lisa took one quick look at her cloth-covered, candlelit table, which was set with Leo's finest china and crystal wineglasses, in which she would serve the Chianti Classico Reserva that the wine-store owner had recommended.

Satisfied it looked perfect, she hurried to answer the door.

At the sight of Alex in a pair of dark gray slacks and a crimson cashmere sweater, her heart began fluttering like a schoolgirl in the throes of her first passion. "You look very handsome tonight," Lisa said, hoping the squeak in her voice didn't give away how smitten she was as she ushered him inside.

Handing her the flowers he'd brought—yellow baby roses with stephanotis—Alex said, "These don't come anywhere close enough to matching your beauty, but they smell nice."

"Thank you! They're lovely."

His eyes filled with a passion that she recognized all too well as he devoured her from top to bottom. "You look good enough to eat, love—different, but in a good way. I like your understated look. It's very sexy, like a beautiful Christmas present that I'm dying to unwrap."

"Thank you again. Now go and have a seat in the living room," she said, needing time to compose herself. "I'll just put these flowers in a vase and get the appetizers. Be back in a sec."

Lisa was back in less than five minutes, carrying a tray laden with bruschetta, prosciutto-wrapped cantaloupe and an assortment of olives. "Hope you're hungry tonight. I've made enough food to feed an army."

Italians never cooked for less than forty.

"I am, and not just for food." He picked up a piece of the toasted bread covered with chopped tomatoes and basil and made contented sounds. "This is delicious. I suspect your lips taste nearly as good."

The determination in his eyes took her breath away, and Lisa wondered how she was going to break the news that she'd gotten her period without upsetting him too much.

It had been a long time between lovemaking, for both of them, and Alex looked as if he was definitely in the mood.

She certainly was!

Damn mother nature and her dirty tricks!

His sexy grin made her squirm restlessly in her seat,

and she cleared her voice before speaking. "Then I guess we've got plenty to talk about."

"I guess we do, love. Look, Lisa, I'm sorry about everything. I—"

She held up her hand to forestall his apology. "Please, Alex, don't apologize again. Everything that's happened between us wasn't your fault. I realize that now. It was just easier to blame you than myself."

"I should never have allowed my parents to criticize you. In that, I'm to blame."

"Yes, I concede that. But perhaps I was too thin-skinned when it came to Miriam and Rupert. Normally, I can take criticism. My parents have been heaping it on for years, so I shouldn't have blown it all out of proportion. Guess it just took me by surprise. I wasn't expecting them to dislike me as much as they did."

"They don't dislike you. They're just old-school Southerners who haven't come into the twenty-first century yet. They've got very odd ideas about breeding and pedigree and all that stupid shit that doesn't matter to me."

"Maybe so, but I shouldn't have run away like I did. I should have stayed and talked things out with you, explained the way I was feeling and given you a chance to fix things, speak to your parents, but I didn't.

"Instead, I took the easy way out. I was frightened— of marriage, of your parents, of what my life was going to be—but most of all, I was scared of losing myself.

"I've finally come to realize that the person you married, the Lisa you fell in love with, was really a very shallow, immature woman, who thought only of fun, having things her own way and living for the moment.

"I never really gave much thought to marriage being a lifetime commitment, or having babies and responsibilities, or being the partner that a man in your situation required. And that was wrong. I was wrong. And for that I'm very sorry."

Alex shook his head, reaching for Lisa's hand. "I appreciate your trying to let me off the hook, love, but you are being entirely too hard on yourself. I fell in love with a free-spirited woman and I tried to change her into something she wasn't. That wasn't right, either.

"My life, the way we lived, wasn't perfect, Lisa. It certainly didn't need to be held up as the ideal. In fact, there were many times when I was growing up that I yearned for a warm, loving family such as yours, who said what they pleased and loved their children unconditionally."

He drew her into his arms then and kissed her, thoroughly and with such passion that the feelings of love and adoration she felt almost overwhelmed her, bringing tears to her eyes.

"What is it? What's wrong?"

She sniffed several times. "Nothing. I'm just so happy at this moment and feeling terribly sad for being so stupid for so long."

"That makes two of us, love. We've wasted a lot of time. I want to make love to you, Lisa. I want to take you into the bedroom right now and make love to you, until we're both exhausted and unable to speak."

"Oh, Alex." She sighed. "Now it's going to be your turn to cry." At his puzzled look, she caressed his cheek. "I got my period last night. I'm sorry."

"Oh." His face fell. "Shit! That means—"

"Yeah. I wasn't quite sure how to tell you."

"So I guess we can't—"

Lisa made a face and shook her head. "No. I'm sorry. The good news is—contrary to what my mother's been telling you and anyone else who will listen—I'm not pregnant. I hope you're not upset by that."

He smiled tenderly and kissed her. "Not at all, love. Now we'll have a chance to really get to know one another. Don't get me wrong. I definitely want to have kids, if you do, but not right now. This is our time to be together, just you and I, with no babies and no family interference."

"But how do we do that, Alex? My family lives here in Philadelphia, and my mother is very controlling—in case you haven't noticed."

"I've noticed, but Francie and Mark seem to have worked it out. We'll do the same. Don't worry. I know how to handle your mother."

"I love you, Alex."

"I love you, too," he said, and they kissed passionately for several moments.

Suddenly Lisa pulled back and began sniffing the air. "*Ohmigod!* I think the lasagna is burning." She rushed into the kitchen and opened the oven, a puff of white smoke billowing out, to find that the top layer of cheese had melted onto the bottom of the oven, but fortunately the lasagna appeared to be still in good shape.

"It's fine. Whew! I don't know what I would have done if the lasagna had burned. I've worked so hard on it."

Walking up behind her, Alex grabbed Lisa around the middle, kissing the nape of her neck and sending goose bumps to every part of her body. "That's good. I'm starving. And since I can't have you, just yet, I've got to appease my appetite in other ways." He palmed her breasts and she moaned.

"Not fair, Alex."

He grinned. "Hey, I never said I was fair."

"We still have a lot more to talk about," she reminded him. "There's my job at the bakery, your new business, where we will live." She sighed. "It all seems so complicated."

"It won't be. We'll be able to work out whatever obstacles are thrown at us. You'll see."

"I hope you're right, Alex. I want our marriage to work."

And for the first time since she'd said, "I do," those many months ago, Lisa knew it was true.

"OH, ALEX," Lisa whispered, snuggling up next to him in bed. "Are you sure we can lie here together and not make love? It's going to be pure torture for both of us. And my willpower isn't what it used to be. I don't mind admitting I'm horny."

Alex caressed his wife's bare back and smiled into the darkness. "Well, I'm game if you are, Mrs. Mackenzie, but I know most women think it's too messy to have sex during their menses."

Menses. Who but Alex would call it that?

"You wouldn't care?"

"No. Why should I?"

"Men are weird. Not to mention that I'm not exactly in the mood for..." He touched her breast. "Well, maybe just a little bit, but I still don't want to go the whole nine yards."

"Whatever you say. I'm happy just to lie here and hold you. Tell me, love, what do you want to do about your job at the bakery? If you like, we can check with Sol and see if he would be interested in letting you buy into the business as a partner, or, if you prefer, we can find another location and you can start your own bakery from the ground up."

Sitting up, Lisa switched on the bedside lamp and looked into his eyes, just to make sure Alex was serious. "You would do that for me?" In that moment, she loved him more than anything or anyone in the world.

"I'm willing to do anything you want, love. I want you to be happy."

Her eyes widened. "Anything? Are you sure?"

Alex shook his head and frowned. "Within reason, Lisa. I love you, but I don't want to be taken advantage of, unless it's in bed."

His grin was sexy, hers mischievous. "What if I ask for a grand house in the country?"

"I'd say you'd have to wait until my business starts making a profit."

"What if I asked for a new car?"

"Same answer as before. Besides, your car is still in good shape because you hardly ever drive it."

"What if—"

"No!" Alex shook his head. "Whatever it is the answer is no, unless, of course, you've changed your mind about making love. In that case, you'd get a definite yes."

"I knew you were only kidding about the 'anything,' but I thought I'd ask anyway." She grinned. "A smart businesswoman like myself always takes advantage of good opportunities."

"You are a smart, savvy businesswoman, Lisa. You've done a great job with Sol's bakery. I'm very proud of you. And I'm willing to do anything to help you get started with your own bakery, if that's what you want."

"The grand reopening of the bakery is next week. Let's just pray things go as well as I think they will. If they do, then I think I'd like to stay with Sol and try to buy in as a partner. He mentioned something along those lines to me the first time we spoke about my working there, so I think he'd be agreeable."

"That sounds fine to me."

"Alex?" Lisa took a deep breath. "I have another favor to ask you."

He sighed. "You don't want to open a chain of bakeries, do you?"

She giggled. "No. I want to get married again. To you, of course," she added when his eyebrows rose. "But this time I want to do it in a nondenominational church, with all of our family and friends in attendance."

"You want to get married again? Why?"

"The first time was kind of a lark. I mean, come on...we were married by an ex–circus performer. Bad luck. We need to be married in a church this time, in front of God and everyone else who matters, so it will be official, a real union."

"I see."

"It will make my parents very happy...well, except for the church part. Mom always wanted me to marry a Catholic. But I figure doing it this way is better than what we did the first time. And I think your parents will be pleased, as well."

Alex considered her request a moment and then smiled. "I think it's a wonderful idea. I'm all for it, love."

"I'm hoping that when I tell my mom that we're getting remarried, it'll take some of the sting out of my not being pregnant. Frankly, I'm worried about how she's going to take the news. She really had her heart set on becoming a grandmother. I mean she practically willed it to happen."

"Your mother is nothing if not determined. I'll say that for her."

"Yes, she is. And she can be as exasperating as anything. But I love her and Dad just the same. They've done their best over the years to make me into a good, decent person. And for the most part, I think they've succeeded."

"Oh, they've definitely succeeded," he agreed, kissing her lips.

Reaching out, Lisa clasped Alex's member in her hand and felt it harden instantly. "Mmm. Someone seems interested. Are you interested, Alex?"

"Stop, Lisa! You're torturing me." He groaned aloud. "It's been a long time, and I don't think I can take too much more of your teasing."

She smiled seductively and whispered, "So who said you have to wait? Just because I'm out of commission, doesn't mean you have to suffer, if you know what I mean. Do you know what I mean?"

As she continued her ministrations, Alex started to breathe hard, and Lisa kissed him with all the pent-up love and emotion she felt. "I love you, Alex, and I'm going to show you just how much."

Trailing kisses down his neck, chest and stomach, Lisa paused.

"Lisa," he choked out.

She proceeded to show him exactly what she meant.

14

CLASPING HER SISTER'S HAND tightly, Lisa sucked in her breath, trying desperately to calm the nervous butterflies beating against the sides of her stomach like an out-of-control KitchenAid mixer.

She and Francie were standing on the front porch of their parents' home, summoning up the courage to go in and face Josephine with the news that Lisa wasn't pregnant.

Lisa had brought Francie along for moral support, but so far, her sister's words of encouragement hadn't made her feet budge an inch.

"Mom's going to be so upset, Francie. I don't know if I can do this." Lisa wrung her hands nervously.

Go figure, but it was the one time in her life that she didn't want to make her mom crazy.

"Maybe she won't be," her sister said, a mysterious smile touching her lips. "Besides, she'll be thrilled when you tell her that you and Alex have reconciled and are going to remarry in a church."

"Yeah, that should go over really well. She'll probably put Father Scaletti on my back and have him harass me for going against my Catholic upbringing. I'll have ~say ten Hail Marys and call him in the morning."

The door opened while the two were still debating the merits of staying or leaving, and Josephine stared at her daughters with a puzzled expression, wiping her hands on the apron around her waist.

"I thought I heard voices. Why are you two girls standing out here on the porch? You don't need an invitation to come in. This will always be your home. Come inside before the neighbors think I'm a terrible mother. You know how Mrs. Cicarelli likes to talk."

"Hi, Mom!" Lisa said, bussing her mother's cheek and trying to look as if nothing was wrong. "Nice to see you. How are you doing? You look nice today."

Josephine narrowed her eyes, gazing intently at her youngest daughter. "What's wrong? You don't usually kiss me and pay me compliments."

Then she turned to look at her other daughter, who was grinning from ear to ear. "What's going on, Francie? Come in and tell your mother everything. Grandma's resting so don't talk too loudly. It's much better when the old lady stays asleep. That woman drives me nuts."

Lisa rolled her eyes at Francie, but said nothing.

They followed their mother into the kitchen and took a seat at the old table, where Josephine placed a plate of chocolate-chip cookies and a pitcher of milk before them, as if they were still little girls who had just returned home from school.

"Don't eat too much or you'll spoil your dinner."

They looked at each other and grinned, and then

Lisa said, "Mom, I've got some good news and some bad news. Which one do you want to hear first?"

Josephine plopped down into the chair next to her, and her hand went over her heart. "I'm not sure my heart can take any bad news right now. Give me the good news first. Then we'll see about the other."

Lisa sucked in her breath, then released it. "Alex and I are back together. We're going to get remarried." If such a thing was possible, since they were still legally married.

Clapping her hands together, then crossing herself, Josephine leaned toward Lisa and hugged her. "I have prayed many nights for this. I'm so happy for you. Wait till your father and grandmother hear. They will be overjoyed."

"Thanks, Mom!"

"I will call Father Scaletti right away and make the arrangements. The wedding shouldn't be too big, but—"

Lisa shot Francie a knowing look. "Mom, we're not getting married in the Catholic Church. Alex isn't Catholic, so we thought it would be better to get re-married in a nondenominational church."

Josephine's forehead wrinkled in confusion. "What does that mean? You want to get married in a church that has no religion? What kind of ceremony would that be? If it's not a Catholic ceremony, it won't be sanctioned by the church."

"It's the kind we want, Mom, and it has already been decided."

"And this is the good news?" Josephine threw her hands up in the air, looking heavenward for guidance. "I'm afraid to ask what the bad news is."

"Mom," Francie interjected, "you should be happy that Lisa and Alex want to renew their wedding vows in church. It doesn't matter what kind it is. You and Dad and the whole family will get to be there this time, and you can wear that dress you bought for one of my first three weddings. You know how you've been dying to wear the pink taffeta again."

Josephine considered the statement. "That's true. But still...I don't know what the Father will say when he hears. He's very strict about such things. I might lose standing in the church, be kicked off the women's altar guild."

"He'll say God bless Alex and Lisa for marrying before God," Francie replied, and Lisa's eyes widened appreciatively, wondering where her sister came up with such good stuff. "That's what he'll say."

"You're right. It's a blessing, no matter the church. So what's the bad news? Do I need to take my heart medicine first?"

"You don't take heart medicine, Mom. You just take baby aspirin, like the rest of the world. It's a preventive measure. You don't have a heart condition," Lisa reminded her mother.

"Okay, so I don't have a heart condition...yet. But you can't trust those doctors. Most of them are quacks. The outrageous money they charge, and for what?"

she asked no one in particular, crossing her arms over her chest.

"What's this bad news you have to tell me?"

"I'm not pregnant. I got my period."

Her mother's face fell, and for a moment Lisa felt terrible about disappointing her.

"You're sure?"

"Of course, I'm sure. I got my period two days ago. I'm not going to have a baby. You'll have to wait a while longer to be a grandmother."

Josephine's eyes filled with tears and she reached for her hankie, wiping them away. "But I was so sure. How could this have happened? *Dio!* We are cursed."

Reaching out, Lisa drew her mother to her and tried to comfort her. "I'm sorry, Ma. I know how much you wanted me to have a baby, but I warned you not to get your hopes up. The good news is that now that Alex and I are back together, I'll probably get pregnant some day, though not right away. We want to wait awhile, enjoy being married to each other."

"And this is supposed to make me feel better?"

Lisa shrugged. "It's the best I can do, Ma."

Francie sat silently, waiting for her turn to speak.

When Lisa looked over at her sister and noticed her grin, she shook her head in chastisement. "This is not a very amusing matter, France. I don't think you should be laughing. Mom's upset enough as it is."

"I'm not smiling about that, you dolt. I have some news that might make Mom feel a whole lot better."

"What?" Josephine wanted to know. "You and

Mark have bought a house in Bucks County and now you're moving away. Is that supposed to make me feel better? I'm losing my girls. I'll have no one left." She started crying again.

Francie waited a brief moment, and then blurted, "I'm pregnant! I'm going to have a baby."

Lisa screamed, jumping up from her chair and hugging her sister. "Oh, Francie, I'm so happy for you and Mark. Congratulations! You've wanted this for so long."

"Mom?" Francie asked when her mother remained silent and still as a granite statue.

Lisa turned to find Josephine looking somewhat dazed. In fact, the woman looked downright catatonic, and she knew immediately that something was terribly wrong. "Mom, are you all right?"

"Get some water," Francie ordered. "I think Mom's going to faint."

And then she did.

Josephine keeled over and passed out right at the table, her head lolling forward to rest on the plate of chocolate-chip cookies.

"Oh, my God! I hope I haven't killed her," Francie said, staring at her mother in disbelief. "I'll never forgive myself, after all the trouble I put her through over those weddings."

"You haven't. Mom just got overloaded with too much news. She didn't have time to digest it all." Lisa patted her mother's hand and soon the woman opened her eyes and lifted her head; there were chocolate chips melted into her forehead.

"Here, drink this. It's water. It'll make you feel better."

Josephine shook her head and cookie crumbs went flying. "I'm fine. It's just such a shock—first your news and then Francie's. You girls will be the death of me one of these days. I've been telling you that for years."

"Then God won't have to take you," Lisa pointed out with a smile.

"Come here," Josephine ordered Francie. "Let me hug you and feel my granddaughter."

"We don't know if it's a girl or a boy yet, Mom," Francie said. "I'm not sure you should be referring to the baby as your granddaughter. What if it's a boy?"

"Oh, it's definitely a girl," Josephine replied with conviction. "Only girls can make me go crazy and light-headed," she said, and both sisters laughed.

"Guess we deserved that," Lisa said, and Francie nodded.

"So, Mom, are you happy now that both your daughters are married and that you're going to be a grandmother?" her eldest daughter wanted to know.

Josephine nodded. "I'm going to church right now and light candles. I will pray and give thanks to the Almighty. And I will make another donation to Father Scaletti, to thank him for his help."

"Father Scaletti?" Lisa rolled her eyes. "What did he have to do with anything? If you want to make a donation to anyone, you should make it to Mark. He's the one who got Francie pregnant."

"Don't be too sure. Prayer changes things. It was God who decided that your sister should have a child, and He made it so. Father Scaletti is my spiritual advisor, and as such, should get some of the credit."

"You may be right, Mom. I prayed a lot over the last few weeks, too," Francie said.

"Yeah, same here," Lisa agreed.

But she wasn't going to admit that she'd prayed *not* to be pregnant, and for her period to be over early so she could have passionate sex with her husband again.

For some reason, she didn't think her mother or Father Scaletti would appreciate that.

"GOD, LISA, I've been dreaming about this day for weeks, only it seemed like years. I wasn't sure how much longer I could hold out. After all, I'm only a mere mortal."

Smiling, Lisa approached the hotel bed, wearing her sexy new outfit. "You like?" She pirouetted about, pleased to see the response she'd been expecting.

"Yes, but I'd much prefer to see you naked. Not that your outfit is hiding much, and not that I'm complaining. You've got the most perfect body and exquisitely beautiful breasts, which I love to admire."

"Instead of your admiration, Alex, I'd much rather have you take these off of me, preferably with your teeth and preferably very quickly. It's been a while for me, too."

"Mmm. What a perfectly delicious idea." Alex made short work of removing the lingerie, then gazed lovingly at his wife. "You are truly the most beautiful woman alive, and I am the luckiest man on this planet."

"And you are, without a doubt, the horniest man on the face of this earth, Alexander Mackenzie."

He kissed her nose. "I won't deny that, but I meant every word I said."

Wrapping her arms around his neck, Lisa pulled Alex toward her and kissed him, deeply and thoroughly, inserting her tongue into his mouth and flicking it in and out, while teasingly moving her hips against his.

"I don't think we're going to need a whole lot of foreplay, Alex," she said in a husky whisper.

Inserting his hand between her thighs, Alex discovered she was wet and ready for him. He kissed her again, and then slowly and torturously trailed his lips down her neck, stomach and abdomen, until he reached the juncture of her thighs.

Lisa felt as if she had died and gone to heaven, as Alex loved her with his mouth and tongue, flicking the tiny bud until she wanted to scream. "I can't take much more, Alex. Please!"

Ignoring her pleas, he kissed her breasts, drawing the nipples between his teeth, and then sucking on them until she groaned. "Alex! Quit torturing me."

"I love you, Lisa," he whispered in her ear as he gently spread her legs and slid fully inside her.

"Oh, my!" Lisa said. "I'd forgotten just how wonderful this felt."

"I didn't," he said, moving deeper and harder until she was writhing on the bed and had to anchor herself by gripping the sheets.

If only it were as easy to hang on to her control!

"Oh! Oh! Oh!" Lisa climbed toward the heavens, coming up to meet Alex's thrusts, over and over again, until with one final push they finally climaxed together and slowly fell back down to earth.

Replete, they collapsed in each other's arms. There was silence, except for the sound of their heavy breathing as their hearts slowed to a normal rhythm.

"I love you so much, Alex. I'm sorry we were apart for so long."

"Shh! We're together now, love." He kissed her forehead, hugging her close. "Let's not talk of the past, but only of our future together. We have our whole lives ahead of us now, Lisa, and we won't screw it up this time. I promise."

"And will you always love me, no matter what?"

Alex leaned on his elbow, propping his head on his hand and gazed into her eyes. "Of course, I will. But are you trying to warn me about something? I'm not sure I like that mischievous smile you're wearing."

Lisa grinned, caressing his cheek. "No, nothing specific. But I'm sure I'm going to annoy you at sometime in the future and I just want to be able to remind you that you promised to love me, no matter what."

"In the immortal words of Billy Joel: I love you just the way you are."

"Oh, Alex, you make me so happy."

"Good. Now you can make me happy by not talking and kissing me again. I haven't had my fill of you yet."

Lisa glanced down to notice that was quite true and grinned. "I think I'm going to like this do-over marriage of ours, Alex. In fact, I'm certain of it."

15

"I CAN'T BELIEVE IT'S all over with."

Lisa leaned back against the bed pillows in their hotel suite at the New York City Four Seasons, and sighed deeply before taking a sip of champagne. The wedding and reception had gone off without a hitch, and she was vastly relieved.

"Me, either," Alex admitted, taking his wife's feet onto his lap and rubbing them. "Your mother was like a whirlwind, running here and there, shouting out orders to everyone. She should have been a Broadway director."

"Get used to it. That's not going to change." Lisa smiled, adding, "I thought your parents were going to come unglued when Father Scaletti showed up at our wedding. The look on their faces was priceless."

"Well, they weren't quite sure if he was there to perform the ceremony or not. My mom's found a kindred spirit in Josephine, I'm afraid. They're both rather manipulative."

"*Rather* manipulative. *Ha!* That's a good one."

"I see your point."

"Well, now we can just relax and enjoy our honeymoon in the Bahamas tomorrow and not have to worry about a thing."

Except Lisa was worried.

Her mother had looked so distraught when she'd waved goodbye to them after the reception. Josephine rarely cried, and lately she'd been shedding tears and leaking like a sieve. It was very uncharacteristic behavior for her mother.

"I know this is a horrendous favor to ask considering it's our wedding night, but would you mind terribly if I called my mom? I'm worried about her."

Alex smiled, stood, and then kissed his wife. "I'll go take a shower and be right back. You call your mom and put your mind to rest."

She sighed. "I love you."

He grinned. "Yeah. And in a few moments you're going to show me just how much."

"I can't wait," she said, reaching for the phone on the bedside table.

It was late, about eleven o'clock, but Lisa figured her mom would still be up, rehashing all the details of today's events with her dad. Her father, of course, would doze off during her recitation and not hear most of what Josephine had to say, but she'd be content anyway, in the telling of it.

Her mother answered the phone on the third ring. "Hi, Mom. It's me, the new bride."

"What is it? What's wrong? Did you and Alex have a fight already? Please don't tell me this. I haven't even paid the caterer yet."

"Relax, Mom, there's nothing wrong. Alex and I are fine. It's you I was worried about. You looked sad when I left, so I wanted to call and make sure you're okay—and to tell you thanks for everything you did.

"The wedding and reception were beautiful. And it was really nice of you to let Leo participate. He's always wanted to be a flower girl." The pansies had been a nice touch, though a bit overt, in Lisa's opinion.

"I'm pleased you liked everything. I got so much experience from your sister's weddings, I'm thinking I should go into business for myself."

Lisa smiled to herself. "So you're doing okay? You're not sad or anything?"

"Maybe a little sad. You're my youngest daughter, Lisa. It's always hard to lose your youngest, even if you were already married. I know that sometimes you find it hard to believe, but your father and I love you very much."

Lisa needed to hear that, and her mom's words brought tears to her eyes. "Thanks, Ma. I love you guys, too."

"When you're a mother, you'll see it's not easy raising a child. There are a lot of decisions to be made about a great many things, and we don't always get everything right. But we try our best.

"Your brother, Jack, has your father to set him straight, so I don't worry about him nearly as much as I worry about you and your sister. I hope you understand."

"Well, Grandma, now that Francie is having a baby,

you can practice some more. Soon you'll have a new grandchild to spoil rotten."

"True. And I'm looking forward to it." Her mother paused a moment, then added, "Listen, Lisa, you go and have a wonderful time with your husband. Alex is a good man. Treat him right and you'll always be happy. The secret to a good marriage is in the sex. Don't forget that."

"Mom!" Lisa's voice reflected her shock. "I can't believe you just said that." She wasn't sure whether to laugh or cry, but she could hardly wait to tell Alex about her mother's advice.

"I never had the talk with you and your sister about the birds and the bees like I should have. I was too embarrassed. But now that you're grown, I figure we can talk of these things and it's okay, no?"

Lisa did not want to ask if her mother and father were still having sex at their age, because that would be more information than she could handle.

Ick! Ick! Ick!

"Sure, Mom. Well, I've got to go and get myself ready for my wedding night."

"Be happy. I love you."

"I love you, too, Ma. Guess I've finally grown up, huh?"

"Who knew it would take so long?"

Josephine always liked having the last word.

"God, Lisa, you drive me wild. If you don't quit moving your hips like that, this is all going to be over with before we get started."

"Can I help it if you give me urges in all the right places?"

Alex kissed her. "I love you so much it hurts."

She reached down and caressed the long length of him, hearing him moan in response. "I love you, too. All of you." She urged him to enter, and when he did, she wrapped her legs about his waist and took him fully within her.

"This is where you will always belong—with me, Alex. I'll never let you go again."

They kissed until Lisa could barely breathe, then Alex lifted his head to gaze into her eyes. "You're mine. I love you. And nothing will ever come between us again."

"Well, maybe something," she said. "And I think it might be *coming* between us right now."

Alex couldn't help but smile, even as he brought them both to climax. "Woman," he said once they'd returned to earth, "you talk too much."

"Yes, but it's part of my charm."

He held her close and stroked her back. "I guess it is, and just one of many, I might add," he said, kissing her again.

"Alex, I was thinking..."

"Uh-oh, that never bodes well."

She knocked him playfully on the arm. "Perhaps we should reconsider our stand on having a baby. I've been thinking that maybe we shouldn't wait, maybe we should just toss the condoms in the garbage and go for it."

Though her comment took him by surprise, Alex seemed delighted by the suggestion. "Are you sure? I don't want you doing this because you think it's what our parents want."

"I'm not. Besides, waiting is for amateurs. We're seasoned married people now. And I think I can manage my job at the bakery and a baby, too. Sol wouldn't mind if I brought our son or daughter into work. In fact, he'd love it. And I can always get Mom to baby-sit, if need be. What do you think?"

"Well, Mrs. Mackenzie, I think we should get started on this new idea of yours right away. I'd like nothing more than to have you as the mother of my son."

"Or daughter."

"That would be fine, too."

She caressed his cheek, letting her hand trail downward to his chest. "This new project could take a lot of time and effort. Are you up for it?"

He grinned, rolling on top of her. "Love, I've been up for it since the day I saw you shaking your butt on the dance floor at Club Zero."

"Then prove it."

And he did.

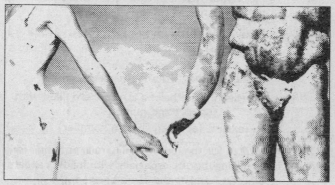

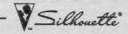

If you enjoyed what you just read,
then we've got an offer you can't resist!

Take 2 bestselling love stories FREE!

Plus get a FREE surprise gift!

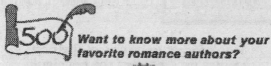

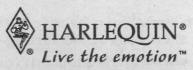